DEVI

Prasun Roy is a bestselling author of several books known for their compelling and engaging narrative style. Two of his fiction titles for young adults have been selected as supplementary reads for the students of Delhi Public School, Vadodara. He has an exciting lineup of non-fiction titles to his credit, including biography, translation, history and mythology. His unique lineup of fiction titles deals with varied subgenres of mystery, paranormal, young-adult and thriller.

Prasun has delivered lectures on his research about unsung heroes at eminent institutions, like IIT Kanpur, Maharaja Sayajirao University (Vadodara), IIT Delhi in association with Indian History Awareness and Research, Defence Research and Development Organisation, Ministry of Culture, Ministry of Defense, Indira Gandhi National Centre for the Arts, Rishihood University, All India Radio and the National Library. He has also delivered talks at prominent literary festivals.

A second-generation entrepreneur—with his family-owned business of pharmaceutical manufacturing and marketing—Prasun lives with his family in Kolkata.

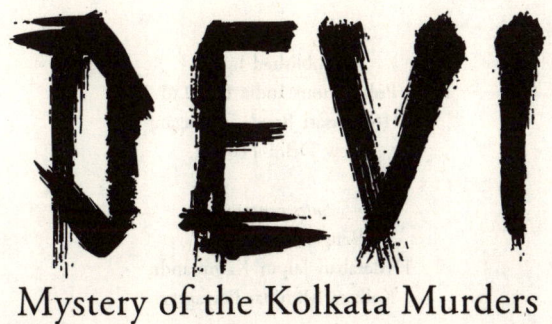

Mystery of the Kolkata Murders

Prasun Roy

Published by
Rupa Publications India Pvt. Ltd 2023
7/16, Ansari Road, Daryaganj
New Delhi 110002

Sales centres:
Bengaluru Chennai
Hyderabad Jaipur Kathmandu
Kolkata Mumbai Prayagraj

Copyright © Prasun Roy 2023

This is a work of fiction. Names, characters, places and incidents are
either the product of the author's imagination or are used fictitiously
and any resemblance to any actual person, living or dead,
events or locales is entirely coincidental.

All rights reserved.

No part of this publication may be reproduced, transmitted,
or stored in a retrieval system, in any form or by any means,
electronic, mechanical, photocopying, recording or otherwise,
without the prior permission of the publisher.

P-ISBN: 978-93-5702-573-7
E-ISBN: 978-93-5702-574-4

First impression 2023

10 9 8 7 6 5 4 3 2 1

The moral right of the author has been asserted.

Printed in India

This book is sold subject to the condition that it shall not,
by way of trade or otherwise, be lent, resold, hired out, or otherwise
circulated, without the publisher's prior consent, in any form of
binding or cover other than that in which it is published.

Contents

Mahalaya / 1

Maha Chaturthi / 23

Maha Panchami / 46

Maha Shashti / 73

Maha Shaptami / 102

Maha Ashthami / 133

Maha Navami / 157

Maha Dashami / 187

Epilogue / 210

Acknowledgements / 223

Mahalaya

The crimson hues of the autumn sun flooded every corner of Kolkata. The city of joy was abuzz, preparing for the biggest event of the year—Durga Puja. It was Mahalaya, a very special day. It is a day that marks the descent of Ma Durga from her abode in Kailash to bestow her blessings on mortal earthlings. Traditionally, it marks the end of Pitru Paksha—the period when Hindus pay homage to their ancestors—and the beginning of Devi Paksha, the fortnight of the Mother Goddess. The silence of a new dawn was broken by the high-octane performance of 'Mahisasura Mardini' being broadcast over radio. The air carried a mild chill and the sweet smell of autumn. The inhabitants of the city were waking up with a festive mood.

At 9.30 in the morning, Police Commissioner Vikram Chauhan entered the VIP conference room on the fifth floor of the police headquarters. He sat down in his seat with an air of concern. Something very critical was about to happen in the city, and that too during the Durga Puja festivities. One by one, a group of high-profile dignitaries entered the meeting room. Within ten minutes, Inspector General Anant Sridharan; Ranjan Mukherjee, the minister of home and hill affairs; Anirudha Goswami, chief of CID, Kolkata Branch; Bikash Talukdar, secretary to the chief minister; and five high-ranking police officers were seated in the room. The video conferencing session began with an equally eminent team in New Delhi, led by the Home Minister himself, along with the chief of R&AW and the CBI chief.

The Home Minister opened the dialogue, 'Durgacharan Mahesh, the business baron, is not unknown to any of you. He is the man behind the multi-million money laundering scam. His business interests span multiple domains, including real estate, pharmaceuticals, finance and hospitality. For the last three years, he had taken shelter in Spain, thereby gaining legal indemnity as per international law. However, our government has fought hard in making a breakthrough.'

The Home Minister continued while the others listened carefully, 'After over two years of negotiations, the Spanish government has agreed to extradite the fugitive from Spain to India. The fugitive would travel through Kolkata before being moved to a high-profile prison in Mumbai. During his transit, Durgacharan would remain in Kolkata for three days. A special hearing would be arranged by a special bench of magistrates within the premises of the Kolkata High Court and an interim judgment would be passed in front of the Spanish authorities, following which Durgacharan would be moved to Mumbai. I know that the time he would be in Kolkata coincides with the mammoth Durga Puja celebrations. I would need your help and support to accomplish this crucial task for the sake of justice!'

Chauhan listened to the rest of the discussion carefully, then picked up the microphone and said, 'Sir, we will assign some of our best men for this task. Durgacharan's transit via Kolkata would be seamless; I assure you on behalf of the entire team of Kolkata Police. We will put up a meticulous plan in place to ensure a smooth proceeding and transit.'

The rest of the eminent personnel present in the room voiced their support one by one and then Mukherjee said, 'We are making arrangements for a secret location where Durgacharan will be put up during his stay in Kolkata. There will be ample security and we will ensure that the peace and harmony of the festivities remain untouched despite his presence in the city.'

To this, Talukdar added, 'Our honourable Chief Minister has given his consent to empower the police department with complete liberty to do what is necessary. On behalf of the government, we would ensure that the media doesn't create any furore around this news.'

Chauhan finished with an air of confidence, 'My team and I will see to it that no unrest takes place when Durgacharan Mahesh transits through Kolkata. We will also ensure that the Durga Puja festivities go on unhindered.'

By the time the meeting ended, a positive assurance gleamed on everyone's face. Chauhan didn't waste any time and immediately called another meeting with his best men.

Inside his personal chamber, five eminent police officers arrived and Jai Pradhan was one among them. Chauhan trusted him the most.

Chauhan briefed everybody about the situation and said, 'We have a task of paramount importance at hand. This will define the efficiency of our entire team, and the honour of the Kolkata Police Department is at stake. We all know that the Durga Puja celebrations are imminent, and we have the gigantic task of maintaining law and order in the city during the festivities. I have selected you, some of my best men, to accomplish an equally massive task. The transit of fugitive businessman Durgacharan Mahesh through Kolkata is a high-security and critical job, and we have been entrusted by the Home Ministry to ensure his safe passage after an interim trial. The Spanish authorities will escort the fugitive and we have to ensure that nothing goes wrong. This is a matter that has gained international importance.'

He continued, 'Durgacharan will arrive in the city on the evening of Maha Panchami. We have to house him in a secured location for the next day. Thereafter, a special court session will be held on the day of Maha Shaptami, and then he will be taken to Mumbai on Maha Ashtami. Let us make a solid plan to ensure that the transition can take place as smoothly as possible.'

Jai uttered, 'Sir, the news of Durgacharan's arrival in Kolkata has already gone viral. Media is already cooking up different theories. We have to be very cautious about everything. There should not be any panic among people during the festival.'

'The exact location of Durgacharan should not be revealed

to anybody. At any point of time, his exact location would only be known to the six of us and the core team in Delhi. This information must not get leaked to the media or to anybody else. I will take care of the media personnel myself and request them to keep things under control at their end,' Chauhan reminded everyone present.

The next two hours went by discussing various aspects of how everything would be handled and Chauhan giving detailed instructions regarding the responsibilities of each of his five trusted officers. The duties and backup options were chalked out and noted meticulously. Yet, deep within his heart, Chauhan missed the wit and sharp intelligence of one man whom he had groomed.

Inspector Arun Palit was a man whom he had considered as one of his best. Though he missed the officer who had unmatched skills, he no longer trusted him. Chauhan sighed and looked at Jai. Arun might have left, but here was another officer who had developed into a fine officer. Chauhan knew he could trust him.

The meeting ended and the officers dispersed. Only Chauhan stayed behind. He sat in his chair, pondering over how to utilize his team members to their maximum capacity during Durga Puja. He crossed his fingers and prayed for strength.

∞

In the darkness of the night, a man walked towards the Records Room of the Police Archives in Bhowanipore. The CCTV camera inside the room had gone kaput since evening. It was the night before Mahalaya, and most of the officers had already left. At 10.30 p.m., only Constable Ujjwal Roy sat on a chair inside the security room, watching a movie on his mobile phone. The unknown man opened the door of the Documents Room using a key and stealthily walked inside. He reached for the cupboards and cautiously took out a pocket torch.

As the light flashed, the outline of the shadowy figure became clearer. It was a six-feet-tall man, with an athletic built, probably in his mid-thirties. He had a sunburned complexion and a hardened countenance with large eyes and a sharp nose. His hair was cut short and his head moved in a restless manner while searching for something. The room was completely dark but for the light of the torch. The man flipped through the pile of old records with his thin and long fingers. He patiently skimmed through document after document from specific lots inside the cupboard. He also went through some of the files kept inside the wall-cabinet. It was apparent that he was looking for something specific.

The search continued for the next forty-five minutes and then the man uttered a soft sigh, 'Devi…'

As the man came out from the room and headed towards the staircase, he shuddered. Ujjwal was standing right in front of him. None of them moved for a minute, and only their eyes met. There was a momentary pause for a few seconds.

Finally, Ujjwal said, 'Arun Sir, did you find what you were searching for?'

Arun broke his silence with a smile and said, 'I think I have found it. Thanks brother for helping me…'

He placed a five-hundred rupee note in Ujjwal's pocket and continued, 'This is not a bribe, Ujjwal. This is for your daughter. Buy her a Durga Puja gift on my behalf. Thank you again for helping me. Now go and ensure the CCTV camera inside the room is functional again. Otherwise, the senior officers will suspect something.'

Ujjwal answered with a question, 'Sir, what is it that you are looking for? Would you like to look up the computer data in the main server room?'

'Ujjwal, I cannot reveal the secret to you now. It is something important for the sake of this city,' said Arun. 'I won't access the computer server. The chief of IB has a special mechanism wherein he receives an SMS as soon as somebody opens that computer. This is the reason why I had to look through the physical archives. Goodnight now. I will tell you everything at the right time.'

The city did not seem frazzled; it was unaware of any danger looming large. Arun hurried back home and decided to meet Commissioner Chauhan the following day. Only seven days were left before the mega festivities began on Maha Shashti. The riddle, one only Arun knew about, needed to be solved soon.

The next two days were uneventful; Chauhan was unavailable in the city due to urgent work in the districts. On the third day after Mahalaya, Arun managed to get a five-minute appointment with him. Meeting the Commissioner of Police was not a difficult task for an officer of Arun's stature; he had been suspended since the last few months. He had been caught red-handed for taking bribe and had been charged with accusations of multiple cases of falsehood and being drunk on duty. Once a favourite of Chauhan, Arun was now abhorred by him, who held dignity and honesty beyond everything else. Chauhan had suspended Arun and had arranged for a trial. The hearing of the trial was scheduled to take place right after the Durga Puja festivities.

'Arun, what do you want now?' Chauhan asked with a sense of irritation. He didn't want to waste his time discussing anything with a dishonest officer.

Arun saluted his senior and began to speak, 'Sir, I know you are disappointed in me. However, there is something I want to tell you and it is really important!'

Chauhan returned an irritated look while Arun continued, 'Sir, I have found a sinister connection between Durgacharan Mahesh and the city of Kolkata! We must dig into it. Unless something is done about it, I fear something grave might happen when he is here in the city.'

The telephone on Chauhan's desk started ringing loudly. It was apparent that the person on the other side of the call was someone eminent. After disconnecting the call, Chauhan got up from his seat with a sense of urgency and said sternly before leaving, 'Arun, don't worry about this city! There are many honest officers who would protect it. Now go home and let me work! I don't need dishonest officers like you around me. I cannot put my trust in you anymore until your trial is over. And please, don't mess with the Durgacharan case. Let my team handle a smooth transit of the fugitive. I don't want to bring in any fresh trouble during the festivals!'

Chauhan stormed out from his chamber and Arun stood there helplessly without getting a chance to speak any further. Feeling dejected, he walked out of the room. As he reached the staircase, Arun met Jai, his estranged mate, who was once his best buddy. Jai looked at Arun and asked him to join him for a cup of tea in the canteen. Arun was determined not to reveal anything to Jai but couldn't refuse the invitation. The two of them went ahead to the canteen and sat in a corner. Jai ordered two cups of tea for them.

Sipping from his cup of tea, Jai said, 'Arun, don't brood over what has happened. I know it is difficult, but you stooped to taking bribes and being drunk on duty. Your present state is the result of your actions. Please try to overcome your past and make a fresh start. Face your trial and then plead to rejoin your duty. You were one of the finest officers of the police department and the blue-eyed boy of Commissioner Chauhan. Yet, look at what you have done to yourself! Please rethink your conduct and redeem yourself.'

Arun didn't respond. Jai's words brought back memories of a dark past that had been a burden upon him for the last two years. He nodded his head, finished his tea and went away. Throughout the day, Arun remained in a state of dejection. He roamed around aimlessly in the streets of Kolkata, which was buzzing and throbbing with multitudes of people. Yet, a strange loneliness held Arun in its clutches, like a dark web, from which he was unable to come out. After gulping down an entire bottle of whisky, he returned home in an intoxicated state. He threw himself on his bed and closed his eyes, wishing to fall asleep and escape from the nightmare.

∞

The rays of sunlight floated in the air like waves in the ocean. The breeze carried a sweet fragrance and the distant rhythmic sounds of a drum charged the atmosphere with a festive symphony. Arun opened his eyes and listened to the cheerful giggle of a familiar female voice. It was the voice of Radha, his wife. She was happy as she awaited the arrival of their first child. Arun's eyes searched for Radha but could not find her. Only her voice reverberated in that dreamy haze. Was it a hallucination or reality? Arun was unable to fathom. He felt happy feeling her presence. But then… there was a pause. The pause was soundless and hollow, and Arun felt claustrophobic. There was a bright flash of light followed by an enormous explosion that shook everything around him. There was smoke everywhere and Arun struggled to come out of it. The very next moment, he saw Radha's lifeless body lying on the floor.

Arun was rudely brought back to reality. He sat up on his bed, sweating profusely. He gasped for breath and then drank half a bottle of water. As his breathing stabilized, he understood that he had dreamt the same nightmare that had been haunting him for the past two years. He was all alone in his two-bedroom apartment and it was 7.30 in the morning. He covered his face with his palms and wept. 'Why did you leave me, Radha? I miss you so much! I miss our child! I don't want to live anymore…' he cried, trying to look for an answer that was perhaps never to be found. Just then the telephone rang and Arun wiped his tears off before picking up the receiver.

At 11.30 a.m., Jai met Arun at a restaurant in Chowringhee, a well-known neighbourhood of Central Kolkata. Arun had requested him to come urgently for a highly confidential discussion.

'Jai, please trust me,' said Arun, 'I have a strong intuition that Durgacharan Mahesh has a very sinister connection with this city. If the issue is not handled before he is here in Kolkata, something grave might happen during Durga Puja! I need your help to solve this riddle.'

'I don't understand. What do you want, Arun?' asked a puzzled Jai.

'Give me access to the police archives and help me rejoin my duty as a police officer!' exclaimed Arun. 'I will be able to solve this critical case. Or else, the wrath of Devi will destroy the peace!'

Jai was taken by surprise and said in an alarmed voice, 'What did you say? Who is Devi? Please tell me everything…'

Arun hesitated but Jai insisted. Being unable to keep it from him any longer, Arun said, 'I have been getting these phone calls from an anonymous person. I couldn't track down the phone numbers, as every time the call comes from a different number and lasts only a few seconds…'

Devi

'Please continue,' said Jai. 'Tell me everything.'

'The phone numbers are all masked and come via a dynamic IP. The anonymous caller claims to be a well-wisher. The voice speaks disparagingly against Durgacharan Mahesh and proclaims him as a demon!' replied Arun, 'The voice persistently warns me that a grave danger is about to befall on our city. Only Devi can do justice!'

'Who is this person? Is it a male or a female voice? And who is Devi? Why did the anonymous person contact you?' Jai inquired.

'It is always a male voice,' answered Arun. 'But I don't know who Devi is or why it was I who received the phone calls. Moreover, the phone numbers vanish from my phone within minutes after I receive them. That is the reason I want to investigate it further...'

Jai stared at Arun for quite some time and then said, 'Arun, I think your daily dose of alcohol has quadrupled. You are hallucinating during daytime as well. Nobody, other than you, has heard the voice of this anonymous person. The phone numbers aren't there in your call list either. How is this possible? I cannot convince Commissioner Chauhan to reinstate you in active duty,' he looked at Arun, into his eyes, and added, 'Brother...overcome your past. Forget your grief and return to normal life. There is nobody named Devi. This is all your imagination. If you agree, I can take you to a rehab.'

Arun got up and angrily said, 'Thanks Jai, but I am not mad. Have a good day!'

Mahalaya

Jai sat on the bench while Arun vanished amid the milling crowd. Jai wondered about his old pal, who now seemed so estranged from the entire world, and sighed, 'Oh, cruel destiny!'

For the rest of the day, Jai remained busy along with the four other officers who had been entrusted with the task of ensuring the safe transit of Durgacharan Mahesh. The team chalked out names of five different locations where Durgacharan could be housed during his three-day stay in the city. Until the last moment, nobody would have the complete information about where Durgacharan would actually be staying. The reigning government had done their best to bring this high-profile criminal back from Spain under the condition that he would be treated humanely. Spanish government officials were to also accompany the extraditing entourage and ensure that the trial and the subsequent imprisonment were not inhumane and that there were no human rights violations. Knowing Durgacharan's illegal activities, he was bound to have many enemies in the country. There would be many who would be after his life as well. Thus, Chauhan and his team had a huge job of maintaining peace and order.

∞

The streets of Kolkata were already draped in multi-coloured festoons and hoardings. The designer-themed pandals stood at almost every corner of the city, looking like palatial structures. The entire cityscape was architecturally transformed into a fusion of modern era and the Middle Ages. Only two more days remained before Maha Shashti, the commencement of Durga Puja. The joy and excitement in people's hearts were clearly visible, as the idol of the goddess and her children could be seen arriving at various pandals. This, too, was a mammoth task, as the sky-high idols were transported to their respective destinations and placed carefully within the pandals. The police played a vital role in the placing of these idols.

Meanwhile, Chauhan ensured that there were no traffic snarls across the city. In the next two days, lakhs of men, women and children would arrive in Kolkata and the city would be bombarded with human activity. It was Chauhan and his department's responsibility to maintain peace and security while every corner of Kolkata transformed into something like a fully loaded local train compartment, where people shove each other, even to move an inch! None of this could diminish the grandeur of the festivities people were looking forward to.

At four in the afternoon, Chauhan attended a meeting with eminent members from media. The meeting had been organized by the secretariat of the chief minister and was being attended by the chief minister himself. Also present were Inspector General Anant Sridharan, Ranjan Mukherjee, the minister of home and hill affairs, and Chauhan. The agenda of the meeting was to sensitize the print and broadcast media about the importance of the safety and security of the city during Durga Puja, while urging them to dilute any hype about the transit of Durgacharan Mahesh. Any unnecessary propaganda about him was bound

Mahalaya

to create pointless unrest amid the festivities. The hour-long meeting ended on a satisfactory note and all the parties concerned agreed to keep things under control.

As evening fell and the hands of the clock reached six, Chauhan sat in his cabin with Jai, while having tea. His head was throbbing after a day of brainstorming. Jai wanted to tell him about his meeting with Arun but refrained from doing so. Just when the duo finished their tea and Chauhan leaned back on his chair, the telephone rang. He picked up the receiver and listened to the voice from the opposite end. He didn't speak but responded with a brief acknowledgement. Finally, he ended the call before saying, 'Okay, my team is coming.'

Jai felt worried, as he could sense anxiety on the Commissioner's face. After disconnecting the phone, Chauhan said, 'Jai, there is bad news. There has been a murder! It is the last thing I expected would happen in the present scenario!' Jai became alert upon hearing these words, while Chauhan continued, 'The city's high-profile business tycoon, the famous builder and real estate developer, Vasudeva Patel, has been murdered!'

Jai stood up from his seat as Chauhan went on relaying the details, 'He was alone in his apartment at New Alipore. His family is in Mumbai on a holiday. About fifteen minutes ago, his secretary arrived to meet him and found the apartment's door unlocked from inside. He entered the apartment and found Vasudeva lying in a pool of blood on the living room floor.'

Chauhan paused for a while, looked at Jai and said, 'Jai, rush to the murder scene. I want you to take up this case.

Remember, this is a very high-profile case. Vasudeva Patel was a rich and influential person in this city. His murder lands us in a shaky situation. We have to handle it very sensitively. There would be people from the media as well; you need to handle them calmly. Keep me informed about the situation. Take two of your trusted aides and head straight to the crime scene.'

Jai rushed out from the Commissioner's chamber. He instructed Sub-Inspector Manoj Paul and Sub-Inspector Sushil Gandhi to accompany him, and the trio hurried in their police van. The latter informed the forensic team and the ambulance to reach the crime scene.

Chauhan sat alone inside his room, trying to figure out what was happening. Was this an indication of an upcoming curse? Was this murder a precursor to something more deadly? Or was it a simple coincidence? The shrewd officer tried to calm his agitated mind and think rationally about the incident.

Jai arrived at the Royal Plaza Apartment in twenty minutes and reached the fifth-floor apartment that had belonged to Vasudeva Patel. The plush apartment complex reflected grandeur and wealth from every corner. As Jai and his two sub-inspectors entered the apartment, they met with the officer-in-charge of the local police station, Sujoy Samaddar. Vasudeva's secretary, Sunil Patkar, stood at a corner with a scared and bewildered look. Sujoy said, 'Mr Sunil was Mr Vasudeva's secretary. He was the first witness. He informed the security guard about the murder and summoned us. We arrived and secured the place. Everything is untouched.'

Jai walked up to the victim's body, which was still lying in a pool of blood, at the foot of a huge mahogany center table. Beside the body written in blood, was the word 'Devi'. The victim was lying flat on his back with his hands stretched out. There was a clear expression of shock on his face. A mass of clotted blood under the victim's head revealed that the back of the skull had been fatally shattered. Three gaping wounds on his chest had been inflicted by some sharp object.

Jai shuddered. He was unable to believe his eyes. His immediate instinct was to call Arun, but he stopped himself from doing so. His mind was abuzz with a plethora of questions, 'Devi? What did this word have to do with Vasudeva? How did Arun know about this word? Does he really know about something sinister that is about to happen?'

Jai turned towards Sunil and asked, 'Do you see this writing? This name here is written in blood! Have you ever heard of it in the past?'

Sunil was too shocked to notice the word. Sujoy replied that though he had seen the word, he had been waiting for Jai to arrive and take over the investigation.

Sunil added, 'I never heard of this name from Mr Vasudeva or his family. I don't know what it means. I don't see how this word can be related with my employer. I am not aware of any link.'

The forensic team arrived and immediately sprang into action. They collected their necessary samples and clicked relevant photographs of the crime scene. Their team lead mentioned, 'See, there are three prominent ruptures on the victim's chest. The three wounds at intervals are almost in a straight line. They seem to be made by some sharp weapon.'

Then, the body was wrapped in a white shroud and taken down to the police ambulance. It seemed that a hard object had been used to make a forcible impact on the victim's head and then another sharp object had been pierced thrice into his chest. However, no murder weapon was found. The murderer had done a meticulous job and had even dared to leave a message. Jai and his team did their due diligence, following which he asked the two sub-inspectors to seal the apartment and place two policemen at the entrance. A few reporters had already arrived and some of the neighbours flocked around the main entrance, shock writ large upon their faces.

Addressing the gathered media persons, Jai spoke in a composed voice, 'We have secured the place. The victim's body is being taken for autopsy. We are informing Mr Vasudeva's family about the incident. I sincerely request you all to not panic. We will do our best to solve this case as soon as possible. The Commissioner of Police is also personally looking into the matter. The truth will be revealed soon.'

As he drove down to the police headquarters, Jai's mind was whirling with many questions. He wanted to meet Arun. He sent a text to Arun and asked him to meet at midnight. He was feeling bothered by what Arun had told him earlier.

After much thinking, Jai decided not to tell anything to Commissioner Chauhan; he wanted to meet Arun first and understand the matter further. Some questions kept troubling him: Why does this anonymous person contact Arun? Who is Devi and how is it related to Durgacharan Mahesh? Where does Vasudeva Patel fit in this scenario? What else is about to happen and how can it be stopped?

Within a few minutes, Jai received a reply from Arun, `'Sorry Jai. Cannot meet you tonight. I am chasing a potential lead. I will meet you tomorrow. Please wait till then.'`

Jai flipped his mobile phone shut in anger and closed his eyes. As he reached the police headquarters, Jai headed straight to the Commissioner's chamber. It was ten in the night and Chauhan was waiting patiently to meet him. Jai entered the room and related the entire story to him. He skipped the portions that involved Arun, as he wanted to be sure of a few things before opening a can of worms.

Chauhan breathed a deep sigh and said, 'Jai, I want you to know something… I guess it is a significant piece of information. Vasudeva Patel was the brother-in-law of Durgacharan Mahesh!'

'What!' Jai exclaimed and stood up from his chair. 'So, this murder does have a connection with Durgacharan Mahesh. Sir, do you think there would be any complications in the extradition of the fugitive while he transits through Kolkata?'

'Yes!' replied Chauhan. 'This case might get tricky. Durgacharan is set to arrive soon. We need to be extra cautious. I don't want any mishap. We must not let any problems arise. Right now, we are groping in the dark for a cue. However, I am sure we will be able to see a ray of light soon.'

That night, with special permission from the Commissioner, Jai and the two sub-inspectors went to check the police archives in Bhawanipur. They spent almost four hours trying to uncover any link between Durgacharan and the name 'Devi'. However, hours of search led to nothing.

Jai sat down on a creaky chair and groaned, 'I don't see any light in the darkness! There is nothing related to the word 'Devi' in any case. I can't even find anything significant related to Durgacharan Mahesh! This mystery is getting deeper and deeper.'

Just then, Manoj came and said something that caught Jai's attention, 'Sir, some files from the document archives are missing! There are no records of them in the computer server either. I was checking the files and their sequence numbers. I suddenly observed that some files are not there!'

Jai replied excitedly, 'Which files are missing? Do you have any clue about their cases?'

'No, Sir,' said Manoj. 'The files are not organized in a manner that can help us ascertain what was present in the file. However, the room from where these files went missing was a store for case files that were two to five years old... Moreover, I even searched the computer server archives of the local police stations. None of the details about these cases are available there either! The data has been meticulously erased from all possible sources. I don't know whether the missing cases contained anything specific to what we are searching for, but it surely raises an alarm.'

Jai again sighed and got up. 'We would have to notify the IB about it. There has to be a separate probe into this matter.

Mahalaya

We cannot handle it on our own. It is almost dawn. Let us go home and get some sleep. We would have more work to do tomorrow. I have an intuition that more events are likely to take place. We need to be prepared for the unknown...'

The three police officers left. As the first rays of light appeared in the horizon, Jai could feel the rush of adrenaline through his veins and the clouds of questions started swirling in his mind again. There were just two days left before Durga Puja and one day before Durgacharan's arrival in the city. He made a brief phone call to Commissioner Chauhan and informed him about their futile mission.

As he reached home, it was almost five in the morning. Jai took out his mobile phone and kept it on the bedside table. He was a bachelor and lived alone in a rented apartment. He then took out some cold food from the refrigerator and gulped it all down with water. As he lay down on his bed, exhausted, the phone beeped. It was an SMS. He picked up the phone lazily and opened the text message. It was from Arun. `Hi, let us meet at the English Café in Park Street tomorrow at 9.00 a.m. I have received another phone call from the anonymous number. It is like a precursor to a crime about to occur. I will tell you everything tomorrow.'

Jai replied with a short `OK' and kept his phone aside. He was too tired to think of anything further. Soon, the sweet oblivion of sleep took him in its hold. A new day had already started to unfold and nobody knew what it had in store. Specks of cloud gathered in the sky, perhaps as a divine indication that something was about to happen and the mystery was only about to deepen in the days to come.

Maha Chaturthi

Commissioner Chauhan sat with the deputy commissioner of the traffic police department and discussed the details of how the department would operate during the Durga Puja festivities. Every year, the entire team of the traffic police department remains on high alert during all the days of the festival, ensuring smooth movement of traffic and people. Chauhan and the deputy commissioner meticulously chalked out the plans for the upcoming days.

At the back of his mind, Chauhan was worried about the high-profile fugitive and his three-day stay in the city. Moreover, the murder of the latter's brother-in-law had added more twist to the tale, even though Chauhan was still unsure whether the murder had any connection with the arrival of Durgacharan.

'Tomorrow evening Durgacharan Mahesh will arrive in Kolkata,' he added. 'A special Air India flight will bring him. I will need a convoy to escort him to a location where he will stay for the next three days. Meanwhile, the representatives of the Spanish government have to be taken to the Circuit House. They will stay there during the trial. Remember, only I and my team of five men would have the information about which car Durgacharan will take. This is a high-security extradition and I don't want any mishap.'

The deputy commissioner took his orders and left the room. Chauhan sat back and looked at his watch. It was 9.40 in the morning. Outside his window, he could see cotton-like cumulus clouds gathering in the sky. The faint sound of an old Bengali song could be heard. Perhaps, it was coming from a distant loudspeaker being played at some pandal. Being in the police department, he had never really got an opportunity to celebrate Durga Puja with his family. Duty had always been more important to him. He smiled and looked back at his work desk.

His mind drifted to the Vasudeva Patel murder case once again. All leading newspapers were abuzz with the news. He deliberated about the progress in the case. He asked his assistant to summon Jai and his two sub-inspectors. Later during the day, he would have to sit with his team of five deputies to chalk out the final steps before Durgacharan Mahesh arrived.

'Sir, Jai Pradhan's phone keeps on ringing. He is not receiving the call. Sub-Inspector Paul and Sub-Inspector Gandhi have just arrived. I have summoned them to your chamber. They will be here in a few moments,' his assistant informed him.

Chauhan was worried for Jai. As the two sub-inspectors arrived, they briefed him about their late-night operation and about the missing files from the archive. Chauhan replied, 'Alright. Now please go ahead and focus on the Vasudeva Patel murder case. I want it to be solved as soon as possible. This would be your prime duty and you two will report to me directly.'

∞

Earlier during the day, much before the break of dawn, when the sky was still dark, something had happened inside the building of Imperial Bank in Chakraberia. The huge British-era building had been the regional branch of the Imperial Bank for half a century. In the early hours of the morning, a man stood outside the locker room. His face was hidden behind a mask and the entire body was covered with a black shawl. In the security room, a man unplugged the CCTV recording unit from the DVR and walked out along with two other security personnel from the room. He was the head of the security team on night duty.

The man who disconnected the CCTV met the mysterious figure at the locker room and said, 'The CCTV recording has been disrupted for now. We are all set!'

The mysterious figure chuckled and handed over a stash of cash to the three men and then went inside the locker room. The man in the mask searched for locker number 333 with a torchlight. Once the man found the right locker, he pulled out a vial containing a greenish liquid and poured it through the lock. Within minutes, the lock melted and he opened the door, taking out an oval-shaped object wrapped in satin cloth.

Then the three security personnel and the man quietly walked out of the locker room.

Before leaving, the man spoke in a mechanical tone, 'Restart the CCTV recording and leave this city tomorrow!'

∞

Jai woke up with a start due to the sudden blaring of a loudspeaker nearby. The local puja pandal committee had suddenly started playing famous Bollywood songs to announce the beginning of festivities. Wiping his sleepy eyes, Jai sat up on his bed and looked at this phone. Several missed calls flashed on the screen.

'I must have overslept!' Jai murmured to himself and got up from bed. Amid the missed calls, there were two calls that drew his attention. One was from the office of the Commissioner and the other was from Arun. Jai looked at his watch. It was almost ten in the morning.

He dialled Arun's number and the latter responded within a few seconds, 'Where are you, Jai? I need to talk to you. I am waiting for you in Park Street. I don't have much time.'

Jai explained to Arun that he had overslept and added, 'I am still at my apartment. It will take me about twenty minutes to reach Park Street. Wait there till I come!'

'I can't wait that long, brother,' replied Arun from the other end. 'I have to leave within a few minutes. There is something that I need to find out. I will contact you soon. Don't worry if my phone is not reachable during the day. I will contact you soon!'

The phone call got disconnected and Jai sat speculating what Arun was up to. He tried to call him back but he couldn't connect. Jai dropped the idea and called Commissioner Chauhan on his mobile phone directly.

'Jai, come and meet me at my office as soon as possible. I need to talk to you urgently!' replied Chauhan. 'Come fast, we have a lot of things on our plate today.'

Jai freshened up quickly and reached the Commissioner's office within the next half an hour. The man was alone in his chamber and asked Jai to close the door and sit down. Without wasting time, Chauhan enquired in a heavy voice, 'Jai, what are you up to? What happened with the police archives search last night? Tell me everything. I have learnt from your team that some files from the archive are missing. I have a very bad feeling about all that is going on!'

Jai explained everything. He revealed about his meeting with Arun and all that Arun had told him, especially about the word 'Devi'.

Chauhan listened patiently and then said, 'Jai, you know very well that I considered Arun one of my best men. However, after the death of his wife, he went astray, and I no longer trust him. I believe, he is making up a fake story to avoid his trial and return to duty! But I will not allow it.'

'I agree with you completely,' replied Jai, 'but how do we explain his prior knowledge about the word "Devi"?'

'Even if he has that knowledge, what does it prove?' Chauhan asked, adding sternly, 'Nothing! Does it give you any clue about the murder of Vasudeva Patel? Does it have any link with Durgacharan Mahesh? Does it give us any information about any upcoming threat?'

'That is the reason I went to check the police archives last night,' explained Jai.

'Does it have any link with the missing files from the archives? No, you found nothing…' commented Chauhan.

'Correct, Sir,' said Jai, 'But we still don't know what was there in the missing files!' responded Jai.

'Even if it is so,' replied Chauhan, 'Do you have proof that they are records about Durgacharan Mahesh or are related to him or Vasudeva Patel or even anything that relates the two of them and would be useful for us?'

Jai didn't have any answer to the questions thrown at him.

Chauhan added, 'The answer is NO!' He looked at Jai momentarily and said, 'Jai, we have to ensure the next few days go as smoothly and peacefully as possible. Everything else is secondary. I have asked your sub-inspectors to work on the Vasudeva murder case. You, too, should focus on the case and also on our plans for tomorrow. I have called for a meeting at two. We have a lot of things to discuss.'

∞

At ten the same morning, Savitri Gupta, a junior journalist at the *Kolkata Chronicle* arrived at the Chakraberia branch of the

Imperial Bank. As she reached, she heard a big commotion and saw a crowd gathered outside the bank's premises. The gates of the bank were still closed and there was a queue of waiting customers. It was clear to her that something big had happened. She took out her ID card, flashed it at the security guard and walked inside.

Savitri was in her mid-twenties. She had a slim built, fair complexion and long straight hair. She was blessed with a face that could melt many hearts. For the last few years, she had been struggling to build her career as a journalist. She had joined the *Kolkata Chronicle* as an intern and had later joined the newspaper's office as a junior journalist. However, she was still struggling to grab a front page story.

As she went inside, Savitri saw the bank manager standing in a corner with a few of his employees, discussing something worriedly. There were no police personnel anywhere, and Savitri's heart leaped with joy knowing that she was the first journalist who was covering this case. She quickly wore her ID card across her neck and walked up to the manager.

'What has happened, Sir?' she enquired in a compassionate voice. 'My name is Savitri Gupta. I am a journalist and also a customer of this bank. Has something happened here?'

The manager replied in an anxious tone, 'Three of our security personnel on night duty were brutally murdered last night! Their bodies are lying inside the CCTV room. Their throats were slit open!'

Savitri looked beyond the shoulder of the manager and could

see a small crowd near the CCTV room. The manager continued, 'This is not the only crime. A very precious jewel-studded conch shell, belonging to a 260-year-old Durga idol, has also gone missing! Somebody stole it last night from our locker room. The CCTV has no record of it. The heinous crime is a black mark on the pristine image of the Imperial Bank! My assistant manager is informing the police for further investigation.'

'There are more eerie things in the locker room…' added one of the employees.

Savitri gathered her courage and sneaked inside the CCTV room when everybody around was busy. Inside, she saw the three bodies that were lying in a dreadful state. She felt bile rise up her throat and quickly went outside, and walked towards the locker room. The locker numbered 333 was wide open. Above it, on the steel doors of the adjacent lockers, she found a word written in blood…'Devi'.

Even amid the gory affair, Savitri was quick to gather her wits. She understood that it was a golden opportunity for her. She made a phone call to her boss and informed him about the latest story that she was going to cover. Within moments, she took out her notebook and began taking quick notes. She went out of the room unnoticed and spoke with all the people present in the bank and took records of every possible detail. She knew that she would have to be quick and complete her job before the police arrived. She secretly clicked some photographs using her mobile phone and offered any possible help to the bank authorities.

Maha Chaturthi

'This is my big opportunity,' Savitri told herself. 'Maybe, my first big break will be during this Durga Puja, as I would become the first person to report this story. A brief coverage, a breaking news, would appear on our online channel. I must prepare a short write-up and quickly send it to the editor!'

∞

The telephone at Chauhan's desk went off. He picked up the receiver and listened carefully. It was a call from the officer in charge of the Chakraberia Police Station. After disconnecting the phone, Chauhan summoned Jai once again. The latter was a little bewildered on receiving the summon, as he had just come out from the Commissioner's office.

As Jai entered the room, Chauhan said, 'I don't know what is going on in this city! Everything seems to be a complete mess. First the murder of Vasudeva Patel, and now a 260-year-old jewel-studded conch shell got stolen from the Imperial Bank, Chakraberia Branch, and three of the security guards were found murdered! Jai, I want you to rush to the crime scene and do some damage control.'

Jai plopped down on the chair in front of him. There was something disturbing in Chauhan's expression. He asked inquisitively, 'Sir, is there anything else that is bothering you?'

Commissioner Chauhan sighed deeply and replied, 'On the door of the locker, written in blood, was the word… "Devi".'

Jai was speechless. He was unable to think of any motive

behind these disconnected incidents and their link with the word 'Devi'. He wanted to find Arun and ask him what he was after. This latest incident was significant enough to at least listen to the man once. Jai got up to head to the Imperial Bank.

'Find Arun Palit,' Chauhan commanded just when Jai was about to leave his chamber. 'I want to meet him. We cannot ignore him anymore.'

∞

Arun stood in front of the massive structure of the Ganguly Palace in Raja Bazaar. The house was a part of the traditional zamindari system of ancient Bengal and the present lineage of the Ganguly family still resided in the house. Even though the zamindari tradition had long been abolished, the current generation of the Ganguly family still belonged to the affluent strata of society.

The palace had become a heritage destination in Kolkata, drawing a huge crowd of visitors every year. The rituals of Durga Puja would be performed with great grandeur and the entire extended family of the Gangulys would flock together in the Ganguly Palace to enjoy the festivities. A special attraction of this puja would be their 260-year-old conch shell, named Bhavani Shankha, which the family had preserved through generations. Throughout the year, the conch shell would be safely kept inside a locker of the Imperial Bank. It would be only during Durga Puja that the conch shell would be taken out and placed in the hand of the idol of Goddess Durga. Arun stood in front of the main gate and stared blankly at it.

'Sir, good morning,' a man standing behind Arun addressed him.

Arun turned back, smiled dryly and replied, 'Good morning, Ujjwal.'

Constable Ujjwal Roy answered in a worried tone, 'What happened, Sir? You sounded pretty anxious over the phone.'

Arun replied, 'Yesterday I received a phone call from the same anonymous number and the caller informed me that a great danger looms over the Ganguly family of Raja Bazaar. Since then, I have been secretly keeping a watch over its family members. However, so far, nothing significant has happened. This morning, I received another phone call from the same anonymous person with the message that the most precious ornament of their ancient goddess is gone!'

'Sir, it is true. This morning, the Bhavani Shankha, the 260-year-old conch shell belonging to the Ganguly family, was stolen from the Imperial Bank in Chakraberia. It was a gory affair and three security guards had been murdered inside the bank!'

Arun was shocked and lamented, 'I don't know what is happening! On top of that, I am on suspension from duty! I wish I was more equipped to investigate this case. I would have tried my best to stop these crimes.'

'What to do now?' asked Ujjwal. He was worried about the turn of events in the last few days. Two severe crimes had been committed and the Durga Puja festivities were about to begin.

'Did you do what I had asked you to?' enquired Arun. He

looked at Ujjwal with an anxious face.

'Yes, Sir. Here are the records of all your incoming phone calls in the last few days.' Ujjwal handed over a bunch of papers and continued, 'These are all masked phone calls that self-eliminate their trails from the receiver's phone. I had tried to trace all of them. However, all my efforts turned out to be futile. Whoever is calling is well aware of how telecom security systems work!'

Arun scanned though the pages, folded them and kept them in his pocket. He said, 'Thank you for helping me, Ujjwal.'

'It's the least I can do, Sir,' replied Ujjwal. 'You were my superior for five years. I have learned so many things from you. You have taught me everything about my work, starting from a regular investigation to accessing the surveillance system. I owe you my career!' Ujjwal paused a while and added, 'Sir, there is something you must know. Jai sir and two of his men visited the Police Archives last night. They were searching for something but didn't succeed. I secretly heard that some files have gone missing from the Police Archives and their records have also vanished from the computer server. Even though I don't know what they contained, I heard that they were perhaps records of some significant cases. Everyone is clueless about what was there in the missing files.'

Arun patted on Ujjwal's shoulder and smiled. Just then his mobile phone rang. He answered, 'Hi Jai…what happened?'

Jai answered from the other end, 'Arun, where are you? Wherever you are, rush down to the headquarter immediately. Commissioner Chauhan wants to meet you as soon as possible!

Maha Chaturthi

Something very important has come up and we need to talk urgently.'

Arun answered, 'I am coming right away!' He smiled and disconnected the phone and said, 'I think my wish is going to come true. Ujjwal, God is giving me another chance to regain my lost honour! Commissioner Chauhan wants to meet me. I hope I get reinstated to duty.'

As Arun and Ujjwal were about to part ways, Arun's phone rang once again. 'Ujjwal, it is again an anonymous number!' Arun said impatiently. He picked up the call and put it on loudspeaker, 'Hello, who is this?'

The voice from the other end said, 'Tomorrow, the Devi opens her eyes! The pagan must not blow the conch shell before that. Save the day or more blood will spill…'

The call got disconnected abruptly. Arun and Ujjwal stood with perplexed faces. Both had heard the warning, but neither could understand what was happening. All the events were disconnected, but somehow weaved together by an unseen thread…Devi.

'Sir, tomorrow is Maha Panchami. It is the day when Durga Maa's eyes are revealed!' exclaimed Ujjwal. 'But what did he mean when he was talking about a pagan? Is the precious conch shell with this pagan? What is the meaning of this warning?'

'I don't have any answer!' groaned Arun. 'I must go to meet Commissioner Chauhan now. I will keep you informed. Things are getting more and more complex.'

Arun rushed and Ujjwal headed back to his duty. The fog

of mystery surrounding the city of Kolkata was intensifying. The pandals were all set for inauguration and the idols of the deities had taken center-stage everywhere. The melody of drums reverberated in the air. However, only a few men in the police department knew that sinister plans were afoot.

As Arun entered Chauhan's chamber, he saw Jai and four other officers seated in front of him. Chauhan said, 'Arun, I have heard everything that you have told Jai. Now I need to know something else from you. What have you been up to?'

Arun tried his best to explain everything that had been happening with him for the past few days. He revealed everything—about the anonymous phone calls, the warning messages and about his cluelessness as to why the phone calls were coming to him! 'Sir, I have no idea why the anonymous caller chose to warn me!' he cried. 'I want to work on this case. Please allow me to rejoin duty.'

Chauhan pondered over his words while the entire room remained silent with anticipation. At last, he took out a piece of paper from his pocket and placed it on the table. Everybody leaned over to read what was written on it.

Devi Durga arrives in the city tomorrow. Yet, this time she will not just mark the arrival of the festivities, she will bring justice to the criminals who deserve to remain under her feet and get trampled. Mortals of this city might face agony, but the goddess will do her duty for the future of all her children.

Devi

'This arrived at my desk an hour ago,' Chauhan said. 'The sender cannot be traced. However, it is a threat that we must take seriously.' He paused briefly before adding, 'Arun, I will allow you to rejoin duty temporarily. However, you will be allowed to work only on this case. After Durga Puja, you will remain suspended until your trial.'

Arun folded his hands and said, 'Thank you so much!'

Chauhan replied, 'Hope your performance in this case is good. You will assist Jai. He will be your immediate supervisor. Much about your upcoming trial will depend on what you do to solve this intriguing case.'

Arun's face became determined as he said, 'Yes, Sir. I will do my best.'

Jai commented, 'My preliminary investigation shows that the throats of the security guards had been mercilessly slit using some very sharp weapon. My team has not been able to find the weapon. We are interrogating people and hope to get some clue soon.'

Arun replied, 'Today, I would like to take Jai and your permission to visit the Ganguly Palace and do a preliminary interrogation.'

Both Jai and Chauhan nodded in agreement. Arun saluted in response and left the room.

∞

Savitri remained glued to her work throughout the afternoon. Her first report on the case had already been published as breaking news on the website of the *Kolkata Chronicle*. She was now a budding star in her organization. Her boss had praised her and had asked her to investigate the case further.

As the day progressed, Savitri gathered some more vital information. She revisited the Imperial Bank and found that the CCTV cameras had been dysfunctional from 2.00 a.m. Nobody had restarted the recording thereafter. She deciphered that the crimes must have happened after 2.00 a.m. She called up the State Police Hospital and spoke with the supervising doctor, who was an old friend of hers. He informed her that the three men were murdered sometime between 4.00 a.m. and 5.00 a.m. Savitri jotted down everything in her notebook. There was something weird about this case: *If the robbery happened after two in the morning, how was it possible that the security personnel were murdered after almost two to three hours? Were these three security guards involved in the robbery? If so, then why did they get killed? Considering that the security guards were involved, the robbery was perhaps completed within an hour... So what happened between 3.00 a.m. and 4.00 a.m.? Is there something more to this case?* All these questions swirled in her mind while Savitri sat and pondered.

After a couple of minutes, she thumped her desk and murmured, 'Two crimes were committed! I am sure about it. The person who had stolen the conch shell is not the same person who killed the security guards. Even though I don't have any proof with me now, I am confident that my assumption is not wrong. I must do something to prove my point. The time gap is the evidence that the two crimes were not done by the same person. It does not follow a logical sequence! This can be the biggest story for tomorrow's headlines!'

It was almost five in the evening when Savitri headed towards the Imperial Bank again. She had hatched a plan. If it worked, then she might recover some facts.

∞

The present descendants of the Ganguly family comprised of three generations. The head of the family was octogenarian Samaresh Ganguly. His movements were mostly restricted within his bedroom, as he suffered from a severe neuropathic pain condition coupled with chronic gout. He was the last of his generation. Samaresh Ganguly had two sons, Akhilesh Ganguly, the elder son, and Pranav Ganguly, the younger. Both Akhilesh and Pranav were in their late fifties, were married and lived in the Ganguly Palace. Both were partners in their family-owned business of textiles. Akhilesh had a son and a daughter—both were abroad for higher studies. Pranav's only son was an engineering student and lived with his parents. Samaresh Ganguly had a sister, Late Susmita Banerjee. Her three children and the respective grandchildren lived in Delhi, Mumbai and Pune, respectively. It was during Durga Puja every year that entire family would unite at the Ganguly Palace and celebrate the festival together. Akhilesh was the unspoken head of the family and the one who had the key to the locker where Bhavani Shankha was kept.

At 5.15 p.m., Arun reached the Ganguly Palace, carrying a written permission from the Commissioner of Police and met the members of the Ganguly family. He had Sub-Inspector Ajit Saha and Constable Bhoothnath Singh with him.

Arun met Akhilesh and said, 'Sir, I don't want to harass the members of your family, but this interrogation is necessary for us to work on the crime and find the Bhavani Shankha as soon as possible.'

Akhilesh agreed to cooperate and over the next three hours, Arun and his colleagues interrogated every member of the Ganguly family. Ajit and Bhoothnath took notes, while Arun recorded the conversations in his mobile phone for later references.

Akhilesh was the last person to be interrogated and as they were about to wrap up the interrogation, Arun asked, 'Was there anything unusual or anything conspicuous about the Bhavani Shankha? It might not be something directly related to the robbery, but is there any incident of relevance? Perhaps, it might help us in our investigation.'

Akhilesh thought for a while and then replied, 'I don't know whether it is relevant or not, but about seven or eight months ago, I met Bikash Talukdar, secretary to the chief minister, at a dinner party. I had known him for quite a few years, and during a casual discussion, he introduced me to a merchant exporter from England who dealt in antiquities. Mr Talukdar asked me whether I wanted to sell the jewel studded Bhavani Shankha. I told him that the Bhavani Shankha was our family's pride and no one in the entire Ganguly family would ever part with it. He smiled and went away away with his companion. I haven't mentioned this to anybody, as it seemed like an insignificant incident. Moreover, I don't know whether this information would help you solve this robbery or not. I really don't think it has any relevance.'

Arun nodded his head and said, 'Thank you, Sir, for your cooperation. We will take your leave now. Our entire police department will do their best to solve this case as soon as possible and bring back the Bhavani Shankha.'

As Arun came out of the Ganguly Palace and walked on the gravel pathway leading to the main gate, something fell in front of him. He bent down and picked up a crumpled piece of paper. Arun looked back and there was nobody in sight.

'Someone threw this at us from the overhanging balcony,' Ajit said.

Arun unfolded the piece of paper and read the note, 'URGENT, call on this number tonight.' There was a contact number scribbled on the note.

∞

That evening, Savitri met the Imperial Bank's manager, Satish Kumar, in his chamber. She had a charming personality that could win hearts easily. Satish was not immune to this charm. The head of security, Rajpal Chaturvedi, and Satish, both were present in front of her, all set for a quick interview. She began by promising that no information revealed by them would get quoted or misused.

After talking for a while, Savitri asked, 'Sir, is there any mechanism by which you could have known how many people sneaked into the bank to commit the crime?'

'The number of times the automatic door gets opened and closed is counted by our central server,' replied Rajpal. He took out his laptop, opened a programme and then said, 'We cannot know how many people entered, but we can trace when the doors opened and closed. The last time the door latch got closed was exactly 3.17 a.m.'

This was a significant piece of information and Savitri's heart started to beat faster. Her calculations were making sense. She controlled her emotions and said, 'Sir, I need one help from you. Could you scan your CCTV recordings and see whether any person entered the premises of the bank yesterday but did not leave?'

Satish and Rajpal stared at each other blankly. This was unthinkable. Moreover, it was a tedious task and would require a lot of time.

Savitri insisted, 'Please, Sir, this is really important.'

'Fine,' replied Rajpal. 'If this helps in any way, I will do it. However, I would need a day's time to verify the footage and scrutinize the videos.'

Savitri smiled with gratitude, 'That would be so helpful. Please take your time. This will surely be a great help to the bank as well as a big step towards solving this crime! I will come back tomorrow and meet you in your office.'

∞

Inside Chauhan's room, sub-inspectors Manoj and Sushil arrived with their initial investigation report. Jai was present in the room and was waiting for some news from Arun and his team. Chauhan had just finished a preliminary meeting with his team of five designated officers who were to escort Durgacharan Mahesh after his arrival in the city. The flight from Spain was scheduled to reach Kolkata at 5.30 p.m. and the convoy of the fugitive was to leave before six. Every detail, starting from the cars, the officers on duty, the junior officers and constables who would be involved in the task, were finalized.

Sub-Inspector Manoj began to speak, 'Sir, as per our initial interrogation of Mr Vasudeva's secretary, we were able to find out that Mr Vasudeva had been setting up meetings with several lawyers across the country. Even though his secretary was unaware what went on between Mr Vasudeva and the lawyers, he could confirm that the meetings were highly confidential. He even confirmed that several lawyers and their juniors had been visiting Mr Vasudeva every day at his residence. The security personnel within the Royal Plaza Apartment seconded this fact. Even on the day of the murder, a junior lawyer had visited Mr Vasudeva.

We have checked the CCTV footage and spotted the man. We tried to find his identity, but we don't have any visual record of him in our archives. The entry register at the Royal Plaza Apartment shows the name as Advocate Anant Sudhakar. We are trying to find this person. He is probably the last person who saw Mr Vasudeva alive.'

Chauhan wore a worried look and said, 'This is becoming complicated by the day! As Durgacharan is arriving in the city, his brother-in-law begins to get in touch with lawyers. However, mid-way, Vasudeva himself gets murdered! Paul and Gandhi, make a list of lawyers who met Vasudeva and ask them about the subject of their discussion. Maybe, we can unearth some facts from them.'

The two sub-inspectors left the room after receiving the command, while Jai picked up his mobile phone to make a call. Within the next thirty minutes, Arun returned to the police headquarters and reported the day's work to Chauhan and Jai. He showed them the piece of paper containing the message.

Arun dialled the phone number scribbled on the note from his mobile phone and a voice answered back. Arun responded, 'This is Inspector Arun Palit speaking…'

A male voice from the other end spoke in a low tone, 'Don't ask my name. I will not reveal it. This phone number belongs to Akhilesh Ganguly, so no point trying to trace the owner of the phone. Now listen to me very carefully…'

Arun had put the phone on loudspeaker. Chauhan, Jai and Arun listened keenly to what was being said: 'A few months

Maha Chaturthi

ago, Akhilesh Ganguly had contacted his good friend Mr Bikash Talukdar, who is the secretary to the chief minister. He had planned to sell the Bhavani Shankha. However, an undisclosed conflict took place between him and his brother Pranav, and the deal got stalled. This shows Akhilesh Ganguly was being covert in his actions. I hope this will help you in your investigation…'

The call got disconnected and the trio inside the Commissioner's office sat perplexed. Three different cases, all of priority, stood in front of them: the arrival of Durgacharan Mahesh, Vasudeva Patel's murder and the theft of Bhavani Shankha, along with the murder of three security personnel at the Imperial Bank.

Later that night, Arun returned home. The streets were empty and he walked up to the gate of his apartment. He had returned to active duty after a while and that made him feel content. As he was about to enter his house, two shadows appeared behind him. Arun turned and in front of him stood Ujjwal and Savitri. The three of them stared at each other blankly for some time. Arun took a careful and cautious look around him. A smile appeared on the faces of all three of them. Opening the door of his apartment, Arun said, 'Welcome folks!'

Maha Panchami

Arun locked the door from inside and the trio sat on the sofa in the living room. There was an eerie silence outside. The time was well past midnight. Arun brought some refreshments to the table and served them to the visitors.

Savitri began the conversation, 'How are you?' There was a touch of emotion in her voice that revealed a mixture of compassion and pain. 'It has been a long time since we last spoke.'

Arun nodded his head in agreement and replied, 'Yes. It has been a long time. My world has completely changed and I don't know if I can ever be the same again.'

There were tears in Arun's eyes. A sudden upheaval of emotion had gripped him. He controlled himself, wiped away the tears and looked at Savitri. 'Anyway, let us start our discussion.'

Savitri continued, 'I learnt from Ujjwal Dada that you are after the trail of the stolen Bhavani Shankha. I am also pursuing the case, as I was the first person to report this. Arun, there is a point that I wanted to highlight to you. This case is not about a single crime. I strongly believe that this case comprises two separate crimes! One is robbery and the other is murder.'

Arun sat up with an invigorated interest and Savitri related her theory about the two crimes: 'Looking at the time gap, I strongly believe that these are two separate incidents. However, I didn't find any correlation between them. I am looking for any clue that proves my theory. If it is correct, I shall be able to give you some more significant evidence.'

Arun clutched his fist in excitement while Savitri said, 'Ujjwal Dada told me that you are back in duty and you are working hard to solve this crime. I am so happy for you, Arun. I cam here tonight so that I could tell you everything I know about this case.'

Arun replied, 'Yes, I am working on this case. If your assumption is correct, then the investigation would take a completely new turn. Thank you for coming to me. Keep me posted whenever you get any new information. And please, stay safe!'

After some more time, Savitri and Ujjwal got up to leave. As Ujjwal stepped out, Savitri took the opportunity and held Arun's hands. The touch of love was clearly visible in her brimming eyes, 'I am still that girl who loved you unconditionally. Even though you might not feel the same towards me, I am always there for you, Arun. Goodnight.'

Savitri went out quietly, while Arun stood near the door and watched the two walk away. He closed the door softly and went inside his bedroom. There was a photograph of Radha on the bedside table. He picked it up, kissed it, then held it near his chest and began to weep. The silence of the night embraced him with its comforting hug and soon he fell asleep.

∞

The morning of Maha Panchami began with great pomp and grandeur. From early morning itself, the organizers of various puja pandals, big and small, were busy making the final arrangements for their inauguration ceremonies. On this day, numerous celebrities would visit the thousands of pandals and inaugurate the festivities. From political personas to movie stars, the list of celebrated personalities would be huge. News and television media would be everywhere, covering the events.

There was an air of festivity and the younger generations were already out in the streets, flaunting their new clothes. The beats of the drums and the blaring popular Bollywood numbers from loudspeakers charged the atmosphere. Footpaths were fortified with bamboo barricades and the number of traffic policemen had been increased. An abundance of street food vendors were cooking their secret recipes from early in the morning, as potential customers could start arriving any time. The five days of mega celebrations and an equal opportunity for business would grip Kolkata during the festivities. This was one time during the year, when everybody, irrespective of religion, caste and creed, would celebrate the festival of worshipping Devi Durga.

At nine in the morning, Arun and Jai sat with Chauhan

to discuss the plans for the day. 'Jai, tell me about our progress on the triple murder inside the Imperial Bank,' Chauhan asked.

Jai responded quickly, 'The murders were committed between 4.00 a.m. and 5.00 a.m. The throats of the three security personnel were slit using some very sharp weapon, leading to the instant fatal wounds and subsequent deaths. The forensic department could deduce this much from the nature of the cuts and the depth of the injuries. However, it is unclear as to how the three men were killed together in the same fashion, yet none could resist the attacker. What sort of weapon was it? Did it strike all three men together? We don't have any answers yet. My team is scrutinizing the CCTV footage and we are trying to decipher some information.'

'Hmm. Keep me posted,' Chauhan replied, mulling over the information he had just received.

Presently, sub-inspectors Manoj and Sushil arrived, and the latter said, 'Sir, we were able to contact Anant Sudhakar about Vasudeva Patel's murder. We will be visiting him right after this meeting. We have also found a list of lawyers whom Mr Vasudeva Patel had met in the last two months. Some of them are in Kolkata, while a few of them are in Mumbai and Delhi. We are contacting them, and we will be collecting their statements today. The murder weapon is still missing. However, the forensic department says that Mr Vasudeva Patel was hit by a hard object on his head. This was a fatal blow and he must have fallen down due to the impact of the injury.'

Manoj added, 'However, he was not completely dead

perhaps. Another sharp object was pierced thrice in his chest to rupture his lungs and heart. Looking at the linear nature of the three wounds, there is an assumption that the second object might have been some sort of a three-pronged weapon!'

Arun sat up. Something clicked in his mind and his eyes sparkled in excitement. He didn't say anything, but Chauhan observed his sudden change in demeanour and commanded, 'Manoj and Sushil, go ahead with the investigation and keep me informed about the progress.' The duo left the room and Chauhan continued, 'What is it, Arun? Is there something that has cropped up in your mind?'

Arun said after a pause, 'Sir, there is something that occurred to me just now. If we look carefully into the crimes, we can observe a pattern…'

Both Jai and Chauhan looked at him attentively, while Arun continued, 'First, Vasudeva Patel is murdered using, perhaps, some sort of three-pronged weapon. Secondly, the sacred conch shell gets stolen. Thirdly, the security personnel are murdered using a very sharp and thin weapon that made impact with a very high speed. And everywhere, we found the word "Devi" written…'

Chauhan asked impatiently, 'So, what are you suggesting?'

Arun replied, 'Perhaps, we can build a theory here. The first weapon suggests a trident, a three-pronged weapon. Second is the robbery of the conch shell. The third weapon seems like a sharp disc, or *chakra*! These are all weapons or accessories of Goddess Durga! And the word "Devi" connects them together! Somebody is trying to draw a picture of Ma Durga using her weapons to prove something. All these crimes are connected via a central thread, which is Devi or Durga!'

Jai said excitedly, 'Sir, Arun has a good point, even though it is not conclusive enough. Unless something else happens that proves this theory, we are still in the dark.'

'Exactly,' said Chauhan. 'Even if this is true, we don't know who we are trying to stop. We neither have a suspect nor a modus operandi; we don't have a clue about the reasons behind these crimes! What is the killer trying to prove? Arun, your deductions are good but we are still clueless…'

'Yes Sir, but we know that one person might have some answers and that is Durgacharan Mahesh! My anonymous caller had warned me. Sir, you would have one day to speak to Durgacharan after he arrives and before his trial. Please interrogate him to find out what is his connection with Kolkata!'

The three officers sat inside the room pondering over what to do next. After some time, Chauhan said, 'Arun, go ahead with your investigation and let me know about any progress.'

As Arun left, Chauhan summoned the other four officers who were supposed to be in charge of Durgacharan's transit for a quick meeting before the fugitive arrived in the city that evening.

∞

Sitting inside the air-conditioned waiting room of the Imperial Bank, Savitri's mind floated away to a time over half a decade ago…

A young college girl, she sat with a scared countenance in a corner of the large hall. Her best friend had been convicted in a homicide case. Tears were rolling down her eyes as every evidence pointed towards Anjali. Just as the constable was about to arrest Anjali, valiant and brave Inspector Arun Palit stormed inside the room and everything paused. It was just a matter of fifteen minutes, and Arun solved the case, beaming with confidence, presenting all evidence to prove that Anjali was innocent. Savitri instantly fell in love with this man, and was completely blown away by his persona! Thus began an untold love story wherein Savitri followed Arun like a shadow, struggling to grab his attention. However, her heart broke when she learnt that he was already married to Radha, the love of his life. Yet, Savitri continued to harbour romantic feelings for Arun secretly. Soon, she befriended Arun and his wife Radha. They were a happy couple who were deeply in love with each other. Radha understood Savitri's feelings towards Arun but embraced her with sisterly affection. Arun, being aware of Savitri's feelings, confronted her one day. Savitri wept that evening and told Arun that she loved him unconditionally and didn't expect anything in return. A strange bond developed between Savitri, Arun and Radha. Over two years later, Radha passed away before giving birth to her child. Arun was left completely crushed.

A knock on her shoulder brought back Savitri to the present. A peon stood beside her and said, 'The Manager is asking you to come inside his chamber…'

Savitri got up and went to meet the Manager. Rajpal was also seated inside the chamber. Savitri greeted them and sat on a chair. Adressing Satish, she asked, 'Sir, any progress with the CCTV footage?'

'Yes, Ma'am,' he replied and switched on the television in front of him and started to playback a copy of the video recording that he had with him; he had handed over the original footage to the police.

'After studying the footage in detail, I noted something,' added Rajpal, 'At 2.00 p.m., a lady arrived, clad in a hijab. Look here in the video recording. It seems that she is quite tall and thin. Her face is not visible due to the headscarf. She is next seen hanging around the cash counters for about half an hour. After that she vanishes behind that pillar. However, we are unable to trace her in any of the recordings for the rest of the day! Behind those pillars are the washrooms. Perhaps she entered one, but nobody seems to have noticed her. We have scrutinized the exit camera recordings too, but we were still unable to trace her exit from the bank. She seems to have vanished into thin air!'

Savitri sat up with a suspicious look, 'Perhaps, it was a camouflage! It could have been a man dressed as a woman. We don't have the answers. However, one thing is sure that she remained within the bank's premises.'

'Yes, Ma'am. This person was inside the bank at the time of the crimes,' Satish commented worriedly.

Savitri replied in an excited tone, 'Or perhaps, she or he is one of the criminals!'

'We should inform the police about this,' said Rajpal. 'It might help them solve the mystery.'

'Absolutely, please inform them about it,' Savitri added as she got up. 'I will include these facts in my news report, not mentioning your names anywhere. Thank you again, the public needs to know the facts. I wish that the police will do their job quickly and solve this crime.'

After coming out from the Imperial Bank, Savitri made a quick phone call to Arun and informed him about the latest progress. She then headed towards her office hurriedly. As she boarded a bus, someone sneaked a small piece of paper in her bag. Savitri was completely unaware of what had just happened and was engrossed in her thoughts. She had been framing her headline and thinking of the story she was about to file.

∞

Sub-Inspectors Manoj and Sushil were completely taken aback on meeting Advocate Anant Sudhakar. The person whom they met and person they had seen on the CCTV camera footage were two different people.

During the course of their conversations, Anant admitted, 'I work as a junior lawyer for the stalwart advocate Mr Yogesh Bajaj, in his firm Bajaj Legal LLC. Mr Vasudeva had been meeting my boss regarding some high-profile case. My job, like the other junior lawyers of the firm, was to ferry the confidential documents and get them verified by Mr Vasudeva Patel. I don't have much detail about the case. However, considering the current situation I am in, I can tell you that they were documents regarding the fugitive businessman Durgacharan Mahesh.'

'We need to meet your boss, Mr Bajaj. Is he in office?' Manoj enquired.

Anant made a nervous phone call and then said, 'Mr Bajaj is in his office. You can come with me and meet him there.' Within the next thirty minutes, the two officers were sitting in front of Yogesh Bajaj in his chamber.

The sexagenarian Yogesh Bajaj said, 'Throughout my life, I have always been extremely cooperative with the police department. I have earned a reputation for that. Today, in the moment of crisis, I will tell you whatever is true. Vasudeva Patel had been visiting me for consultation regarding legal indemnity for Durgacharan Mahesh. As we all know, Durgacharan arrives in the country today. Vasudeva was just another client for me and my firm. He wanted to form a legal panel to fight a court case, so that Durgacharan could get bail after his extradition and retaliate with a strong defense.' He paused for a while and said, 'Anant is innocent. He has nothing to do with the murder. Moreover, he didn't even visit Vasudeva that day. I request you to spare him from further anxiety.'

Sub-Inspectors Manoj and Sushil came out from the office of Bajaj Legal LLC and sat inside a coffee shop. They took out the phone numbers of the other lawyers and began contacting them. It took them hours to interrogate all the lawyers, but finally one thing was clear to the two—Vasudeva Patel was furtively connecting with high profile lawyers to seek a safe refuge for Durgacharan Mahesh. The duo prepared a quick report and headed to meet Commissioner Chauhan in his office.

Meanwhile, early afternoon, Talukdar arrived at the Grand Orchid Hotel, along with his muse Monika, the exotic dancer and movie actress. The duo were the chief guests for the inauguration of the famous Tollygunge Societal Durga Puja. The organizers had booked a room in the plush Grand Orchid Hotel for them to rest and have some refreshments.

While Monika took the room keys, Talukdar said to one of the members of the organizing committee, 'The car should be ready in an hour. We would come down and head for the inauguration ceremony at the pandal. Have you arranged for drinks in the room?'

'Sir, everything has been done. Please enjoy your refreshments and we shall be waiting here for you,' answered one of the committee members.

Talukdar and Monika walked away with an air of arrogance and headed towards their designated room. After entering the room, Talukdar sat on the luxurious couch while Monika made a nice drink of single malt for him.

'Honey, here is your favorite drink…' she said with a smile.

'Thanks, darling!' replied Talukdar with a smirk. 'You look dazzling in this saree! Your beauty is unparalleled. I will make you a star, sweetheart!'

Monika smiled shyly and replied, 'Stop flirting with me! You enjoy your drink. I will go and do my final touch-ups.'

Talukdar took a sip and sat back with a relaxed mood. Monika went to the washroom. As she closed the washroom door, took out her makeup and was about to start, she heard the shattering sound of glass breaking and a loud cry. Even in that moment of shock, she recognized the voice. Monika rushed out of the washroom and shuddered when she saw that Talukdar had been pinned down to the couch by an arrow piercing through his neck. The man was bleeding profusely and struggling to say something. Before she could understand anything, another arrow flew in from outside the window and struck Talukdar through his heart! The man cried out in pain for a while and then lay still.

Monika was in a daze, shivering from the shock. She picked up the intercom and screamed, 'Murder! Murder...' and fainted on the floor in front of the lifeless body of Bikash Talukdar. A gush of blood oozed out from his wounds and filled the floor like a puddle.

∞

Chauhan sat in his chamber with his team and discussed the plans for the evening. Jai would escort Durgacharan Mahesh in a special car. The convoy was set to depart from the airport as fast as possible. Chauhan would himself be present at the venue where Durgacharan would be housed and the exact location would be revealed by him once the cars would start moving.

The telephone at his desk rang a few times before Chauhan picked up the receiver and answered, 'Commissioner Chauhan speaking...'

Within moments, his face was clouded with anxiety, and he sprang up from his seat. The rest of the team looked on, wondering if more bad news was imminent. He disconnected the call, sat down with a thud and declared, 'Mr Bikash Talukdar, secretary to the chief minister, was murdered a few minutes ago inside the Grand Orchid Hotel. I am not sure what is happening to this city this Durga Puja…' He paused for a while before adding, 'Folks…please leave Jai and me alone for a while. I need to discuss something with him personally.'

The four officers quickly left while Chauhan stared blankly at the revolving ceiling fan.

'How?' exclaimed Jai. 'Is there anything else that we are missing out on but is worth noting?'

'Talukdar was inside a hotel room when he was struck and pinned down to a couch by two arrows!' proclaimed Commissioner Chauhan. 'There was a piece of paper attached to one of the arrows… on it was written the word "Devi".'

Jai was speechless. This was the fourth crime within such a short time and was again connected to the one sinister yet elusive thread…Devi! Jai was clueless as to what was the correlation between all these crimes and the word. He gave a confused look to the Commissioner.

Chauhan picked up the phone, dialled a number and began speaking after a while, 'Arun, this is Chauhan speaking. There has been another crime. Mr Bikash Talukdar, secretary to the chief minister, was murdered inside the Grand Orchid Hotel. Rush to the crime scene and take charge. Wherever you are, immediately head towards the Grand Orchid Hotel. This murder is also associated with Devi… Go and find out everything about it. Jai and I would be busy with Durgacharan's transit, so you need to manage everything about this latest crime. Keep me posted about the progress.'

'This is getting extremely complicated!' said Chauhan in a nervous voice. 'Jai, today is Maha Panchami. The Secretary's murder will take the pressure to a completely different level. We have to solve this mystery as soon as possible.'

Sub-Inspector Manoj and Sushil entered his chamber. They presented their report and the progress made in the day. Manoj added, 'Vasudeva Patel was trying to buy freedom for Durgacharan Mahesh. All the lawyers have admitted that Vasudeva had contacted them to find a legal asylum for Durgacharan. However, before anything could be materialized, he was murdered.'

Chauhan and Jai were surprised as they listened while Sushil added, 'The person in the CCTV footage was not Anant Sudhakar. It is most likely that the perpetrator had faked his identity.'

Chauhan commanded, 'Go and find out about the person in the footage. This is the only visual clue we have so far!'

The two sub-inspectors left the room, and Jai, too, got up. The time was well past four and the time for Durgacharan's arrival was nearing.

∞

Savitri entered her office and went inside her cubicle. She needed to pen down the latest story on the elusive visitor inside the Imperial Bank who never left. This person was either the murderer or the thief who had stolen the Bhavani Shankha. She placed her hand inside her bag to get her mobile phone, but out came a small piece of paper. She was startled seeing the folded piece of paper, no doubt sneaked into her bag unknowingly.

With a palpitating heart, Savitri unfolded the note and read the handwritten lines, 'Bhavani Shankha is in danger. The pagans are many. One is dead, but the threat remains. Devi will not let this happen. The evil blade must not auction the sacred conch shell…else mayhem will follow from her wrath!'

Savitri sat speechless for a while. She re-read the lines several times but was unable to decipher a proper meaning. In her confusion, she picked up her mobile phone and called up Arun, 'Hi, Arun, where are you? Something just happened and I need to talk about it…'

Arun answered back, 'I am entering the Grand Orchid Hotel. Something terrible has happened here too. Mr Bikash Talukdar, secretary to the chief minister, was murdered inside a room here! I have come to lead the case.'

'That is unbelievable!' shouted Savitri. 'So many crimes are happening during Durga Puja… Arun, it is really scary!'

Arun answered, 'What were you telling me Savitri? You said something happened…'

Savitri briefly explained the situation to him and added, 'I have the handwritten note with me. I will give it to you when

I meet you. Before that, I will click a photo and send it over to you. I will write down my day's report quickly and head towards the Grand Orchid Hotel. I will meet you in about an hour and a half.'

As Arun reached Room No. 706 on the sixth floor of the Grand Orchid Hotel, the local police had already secured the place. There was commotion all across the hotel, and the staff and security personnel were struggling to control it. Inside the room, the victim's body laid untouched. Arun went inside to take a closer look. Talukdar's lifeless body was pinned onto the couch with two sharp metallic arrows. One arrow had pierced through his windpipe and the other through his heart. Death had arrived pretty quickly, Arun deduced from the nature of the fatal wounds. On one of the arrows was attached a small cardboard piece with the word 'Devi' written in red.

The officer in charge of the local police station commented, 'The arrows came in through that window,' and pointed out towards a large window that overlooked the adjacent main road. The glass had been shattered due to the sheer force of the arrows.

'The speed at which an arrow can break the glass window and pierce through the victim's windpipe is something significant!' proclaimed Arun. 'It must have been shot using some mechanical weapon.'

Arun looked at the officer-in-charge and commanded, 'Search the adjacent buildings and interrogate people as you feel necessary. This must have come from one of those locations.'

Arun scrutinized the place thoroughly and then interrogated

Monika for a while. She was still in a state of shock. After finishing his initial investigation, he left the place for the forensic team to do their job while the body was wrapped in a white shroud and carried out.

Arun came down to the lobby and waited for Savitri to arrive. Sub-Inspector Ajit Saha was with Arun and finding an opportune moment said, 'Sir, the murderer must have known which room the victim was supposed to stay in, otherwise how could he have shot the arrows within minutes of Talukdar's arrival? Moreover, the murderer must have a tremendous aim, looking at the precision with which the arrows were shot. This murder looks very planned. We must interrogate the hotel staff and the puja committee organizers who had booked the room. He was supposed to be the chief guest at the inauguration ceremony of a Durga Puja pandal today. I am sure the murderer must have received information about the room where Talukdar was supposed to stay beforehand.'

'Good point, Ajit,' replied Arun. 'Take two officers with you and speak with the staff as well as the committee members of the pandal where Talukdar was to go as the chief guest. Record their statements.'

Arun added, 'I cannot understand the motive behind this murder and its connection with Devi. Four murders have already been committed and we are still unable to decipher the invisible thread connecting them with Devi. That is the most disturbing part.'

Savitri arrived within the next twenty minutes. Her breaking news about the elusive visitor at the Imperial Bank was already creating ripples across digital platforms. She handed over the note to Arun and said, 'What is going on in this city? Durga Puja celebrations have never taken place amid such violent crimes! I hope everything gets resolved soon.'

Bhavani Shankha is in danger. The pagans are many. One is dead, but the threat remains. Devi will not let this happen. The evil blade must not auction the sacred conch shell...else mayhem will follow from her wrath! Arun studied the note and handed it over to Ajit and said, 'Take this to the forensic department. We need a handwriting expert to decipher whether we have a match with any recorded criminal in our archives. Moreover, we need to show this to Commissioner Chauhan. This is another threat and a new riddle!'

The time was forty minutes past five in the evening. As Chauhan was about to head out, his office mobile phone buzzed with the notification of an email. He hurriedly opened the email to check its contents. It was from an anonymous source and read: `Blood has been spilled and more is coming. The pagans will face their fate. Devi is angry and revenge is inevitable. Do not fear because justice will be done. The weapons of the goddess are invisible and invincible; don't try to stop them. Maha Shashti will usher in more fireworks.'`

Chauhan stood still for a while and wondered about the implications. He was sure that the source and the location from where the email was sent would be untraceable. He immediately called the Cyber Cell Chief, Mahavir Nath, and said, 'I have received this email a few minutes back. Try and trace the sender and the location from which it has been sent. I need to get hold of the person who has sent it.'

Mahavir replied, 'My team will begin work immediately. I will keep you informed about the findings.'

Chauhan needed to head towards the location where Durgacharan would be housed. He got inside his car and instructed the driver. Sitting in the backseat, he pondered, *I have time till tomorrow night. Durgacharan would be in our custody tonight and the whole of tomorrow. If Arun is right, we might be able to extract some information from him. All these crimes are somehow related to this man, even though we don't know how. I am really puzzled about what to do.*

As he closed his eyes for a while to gather his thoughts, his phone beeped again. This time it was a message from Arun. He opened the message and saw the image sent by Arun. It was a photograph of the note that was sneaked into Savitri's bag.

He called up Arun and asked, 'Arun, where did you receive this?'

Arun replied, 'Sir, my friend Savitri is a journalist at the *Kolkata Chronicle*. She is the reporter who was covering the Bhavani Shankha theft case. This note was sneaked into her bag this afternoon. Savitri is here with me right now.'

Arun further went on to explain how Savitri first got involved in the Imperial Bank case and the progress she had made in the last few days. He added that Savitri had been able to extract the information about the elusive guest at the bank, who never went out. He added, 'Sir, her theory might have some merit. Perhaps, the theft was done by one person and the murders were done by somebody else! There is credence to this theory and I shall explain it to you once we meet. Meanwhile, I will continue with my investigation.'

Chauhan disconnected the phone and sat with an even more perplexed face. There were questions whose answers were hiding in the dark. He needed to unveil them and solve this series of crimes that had gripped the city amid the festivities. Enthusiastic people were already thronging the streets of Kolkata. Evening had blanketed the skyline and the streets were glowing with decorated lights. Chauhan's car drove past the crowd and steadily headed towards its destination.

This carnival of peace would not be marred by the fireworks of crime. I will not let it happen! No matter what it takes, I shall do anything to protect the city and the people, he vowed to himself.

At the Grand Orchid Hotel, Ajit interrogated the hotel staff and returned to Arun. He reported, 'Sir, in the computer reservation system, rooms are allotted to the guests when bookings are done in advance. Mr Talukdar's room was booked two days ago and as per his preference, Room No. 706 had been allotted to him.'

Arun stared at Ajit silently while the latter continued, 'It seems that somebody might have accessed the reservation system database. However, we don't have any proof of it.'

Arun listened carefully and then said, 'Alright. Now let us go and inspect the adjacent buildings on the opposite side of the road. I want to find out the location from where the arrows might have been shot. We need to rush and try to form an idea about how the murderer managed to shoot Talukdar.'

Arun handed over his mobile phone to Savitri and said, 'Keep my phone with you for a while. If the Commissioner calls, tell him I will ring him back.'

Arun and Ajit left, while Savitri sat on a sofa at a corner in the lounge. On a widescreen television, the news media was going abuzz with the recent crime scenario that had cast a gloomy shadow on Kolkata. A consensus of the interviewed masses revealed a sense of fear that was slowly gripping the city. Savitri felt uncomfortable. The delight of the festive season was being subdued by the widespread media coverage of the crimes that had been taking place.

Arun's mobile phone started to ring. Savitri saw an unknown number flash on the screen. Unable to see Arun anywhere around, she received the call, 'Hello, who is this?'

A strange voice responded from the opposite end, 'The merchants of Ecstasy and Ice would soon blow the conch shell. If they unite with the Evil Blade, then mayhem would follow! Devi will not tolerate it...'

Before Savitri could speak a word, the call got disconnected. She tried to call back on the number but couldn't get through. Her heart began to beat fast and she waited with bated breath for Arun to return. After about fifty minutes, Arun and Ajit came back to the lounge and Savitri rushed to them anxiously.

On seeing her anxious, Arun asked her, 'Savitri, what happened?'

She explained what had just transpired and added nervously, 'Arun, I think some drug peddler is involved in this dirty game! The message clearly mentioned the names of famous recreational drugs! I don't know how everything connects, but I have a feeling that the Bhavani Shankha might get smuggled via the mediation of some drug peddler in the city.'

Arun replied, 'I think your deductions are correct. Ajit, ask our men to find the whereabouts of active drug suppliers in Kolkata. Tell them to collect the data fast. Activate all our hidden informers. I want the information within the next two hours.'

Arun looked at Savitri, held her hand and said, 'Don't worry. Everything will be fine. Although there is one phrase that I don't understand. What is the meaning of Evil Blade? This phrase was used in your note as well as in the phone call to me. There must be some significance!'

Savitri kept holding Arun's hand, feeling a bit relieved with every passing second. Arun took his phone and said, 'I must inform Commissioner Chauhan about this recent development. He needs to know about this message from my anonymous caller.'

∞

Amid the festivities on the streets, Akhilesh Ganguly met retired Major Digvijay Talwar inside the quiet quarters of the huge lawn within the plush Tollygunge Heritage Club. The duo engaged in a heated conversation. Unseen by any, from behind the shadow of a tree, a figure was recording the conversation quietly.

Akhilesh spoke excitedly, 'This is pure blackmail. How can you do this to me, Talwar? You know I will be ruined. Please don't do this. I am warning you. Don't test my patience!'

Major Talwar replied, 'I am not threatening you. This is my advice. Agree to the terms and you will receive your reward. Nobody will come to know anything. Cooperate and be in profit, Akhilesh!'

'I need some more time. I am in a fix. Please give me a little time!' Akhilesh answered.

Major Talwar finished with, 'The decision is yours, Akhilesh. Being a friend, I have given my opinion. Don't mess with these folks. They can be dangerous. Be intelligent and take what you are getting.'

The two men parted ways. The elusive figure completed the video recording and stealthily vanished from the spot.

∞

At the Kolkata International Airport, the special Air India flight landed at the right time. Mediapersons flocked outside the main gate. It was a big occasion. Fugitive business baron Durgacharan Mahesh had arrived and every reporter wanted to get a photograph for their next morning's edition. The police had already made ample security arrangements. Jai stood in front of the immigration counter with an anxious face. Soon, Durgacharan emerged, dressed in an expensive suit. He wore dark sunglasses to avoid any eye contact. He was six-feet tall, pot-bellied, with a round face that wore a thick greyish beard and moustache. The smirk on his lips clearly indicated the lack of any repentance in his heart. The Spanish entourage of legal and political officials escorted him, along with the officers from the CBI. Jai led the men towards an exit where the police cars were waiting for them. Jai had his instructions. He led Durgacharan inside the third car amid the convoy of six. The Spanish team was boarded on a luxury SUV.

Reporters clicked photographs fervently as blinding flashlights lighted up the area. As soon as the people got in the cars, the convoy sped away from the premises of the airport and headed straight towards the highway. Midway, after about fifteen minutes, three cars, including the one carrying Durgacharan and Jai, took a left turn. The rest of the cars went straight towards the Circuit House.

At 8.30 p.m., the convoy of Jai and Durgacharan arrived at a heavily guarded yet secluded bungalow in Alipore. The men alighted from the cars while Chauhan came out from the inner quarters.

As everybody got inside the huge living room, Chauhan spoke, 'Durgacharan, you will remain under house arrest here for the next three days. Your trial will be conducted during this period and then you will be taken to Mumbai. During your stay here, you won't have access to phone calls or Internet. I trust you are repentant of your deed, so that justice can be meted out.'

Durgacharan replied in a heavy baritone, 'Repentant? Not at all…I know I shall be a free man soon.'

The tone of his voice and the arrogant attitude left a bitter impression on both Jai and Chauhan. The latter finished the conversation, 'Very well then. We would soon see the outcome.'

Jai and Chauhan came outside the bungalow after a while. Chauhan instructed the designated policemen about the security plans and headed out in his car, accompanied by Jai.

'Sir, Durgacharan seems to me a sheer demon! His arrogance is so stark and his confidence is equally startling. He is so sure that he will be able to evade law and escape punishment,' Jai raised his concerns.

'Abundance of money and audacity has created this demon,' Chauhan replied. 'It is a pity that we have to offer him security until justice is delivered.'

The car sped away towards the police headquarters, where Arun was eagerly waiting. Chauhan received all updates from Arun and sat down in his chair in a thoughtful mood. Jai sat next to Arun. Everyone was speechless for some time.

Breaking the silence, Arun said, 'Sir, Talukdar's murder is another example wherein the murder weapon is one of the weapons of Goddess Durga! The theory that I presented to you is making some sense. However, we are still in the dark about a possible suspect and the reasons behind the crimes.'

'We are also unaware of how all these crimes are interrelated!' added Jai.

Maha Panchami

'The anonymous caller had warned us about Durgacharan's involvement. Can we speak with him while he is under house arrest?' Arun questioned.

'That man is a devil,' replied Chauhan, sounding dismayed. 'He is so rude and arrogant. We know we cannot interrogate him regarding this case, and he will never answer our questions willingly. I don't think it is a good idea to talk to him.'

Jai responded with, 'I completely agree with you, Sir.'

'It is quite late in the night now. Let us finish our pending work and meet at my office here tomorrow sharp at eight in the morning. Tomorrow is Maha Shashti and the first big day of Durga Puja festivities. Moreover, the fugitive is in the city, too! We need to be fully alert. If these crimes are following the pattern that we think, something will happen tomorrow as well, and things will get murkier. We need to maintain peace and harmony in the city, and also ensure law and order,' Chauhan added.

The conversation didn't last long. The three men parted ways and went in their respective directions. Chauhan headed to the Cyber Crime Department, while Arun headed for Park Street where Savitri was waiting for him at a restaurant. Jai headed back home. He desperately needed some sleep.

Just when Jai reached home, his phone rang. The voice from the other end spoke in a mechanical tone, 'Jai, the murders of Vasudeva and Talukdar are connected by one invisible thread… the Bhavani Shankha! Visit the streetlight post number 222 inside Rabindra Sarovar Lake Garden sharp at 5.00 a.m. tomorrow and collect the proof of this statement and the clue to solve another crime!'

Before Jai could even utter a word, the line got disconnected. Jai tried to call back but in vain. His heart began to beat rapidly. Questions and anxiety clouded his imagination. He knew he would have to wait for a few more hours before he could uncover anything at the Rabindra Sarovar Lake Garden.

Meanwhile, Arun and Savitri finished a quiet dinner and he escorted her back to her home. As Arun walked away, Savitri felt like running towards him and hugging him from behind. She held her emotions back and went inside her house. Deep in her heart, she could feel her love for Arun surging once again. Arun vanished in the darkness, unaware of what Savitri was feeling for him.

Meanwhile, Chauhan could uncover nothing with the help of the personnel at the Cyber Crime Department, as the email he had received earlier that evening was a camouflaged one. He returned home, dejected and worried. A charged atmosphere of Durga Puja fiesta could be felt in the air. Only destiny knew what was in store in the upcoming days.

Maha Shashti

Jai reached Rabindra Sarovar Lake Garden sharp at five in the morning. The first light of dawn was yet to make an appearance. The wind carried a cool freshness. The streetlights had been switched off and an early-morning haze covered everything. The chirping of birds seemed to be declaring the beginning of the festivities. Early risers were busy finishing their rounds of morning walk. Jai quietly headed towards streetlight post number 222 inside the garden. The lamp post was positioned at a secluded place and Jai looked around it for his prized clue. Suddenly, his eyes fell on something near the base of the lamp post and he started feeling a rush. It was a mobile phone that had been there in such a way that it would be only visible to someone who would closely scrutinize the area. Jai picked up the phone. There was no SIM card inside; he opened the media gallery.

To his surprise, Jai found pictures of some familiar and some unfamiliar people. He could recognize Vasudeva Patel and Akhilesh Ganguly in separate pictures. However, he was not sure about the identity of the other people in the photos. There was a photograph of one man dressed like a gypsy, who seemed quite familiar to Jai. However, he could not recall the man's identity. There was a video recording of Akhilesh Ganguly at the Tollygunge Heritage Club. Jai watched it carefully. He could not recognize Major Talwar in the video but understood that some sinister act had been captured. There were multiple pictures and videos of Major Talwar, Akhilesh and his younger brother, Pranav, and Vasudeva Patel, accompanied by the man dressed like a gypsy. One video that startled Jai was that of Akhilesh showing the Bhavani Shankha to the rest of the men. The audio of most of the videos were of either very poor quality or muted.

What is the meaning of all this? What is the identity of the person who has captured all this and why is he giving it to me? Jai questioned himself. *Whatever it is, these are significant clues to solve one crime perhaps. Maybe, we will be able to recover the Bhavani Shankha and also discover a link to this crime with the Ganguly brothers!* Jai answered his own questions. Without wasting much time, he kept the smartphone inside his pocket and quickly left from the spot.

Unknown to anyone, an anonymous figure had observed the entire episode, smiling.

∞

Maha Shashti

Maha Shashti festivities had started. All the puja pandals had already been inaugurated and people had started thronging the streets from early in the morning. The overflow of traffic and the excess of pedestrians made the city of Kolkata throb with electrifying energy.

Even such gusto could not defy the fact that an element of mystery was shourding Kolkata. The recent murders and the robbery of the Bhavani Shankha were extensively covered by every media group and the news about the arrival of Durgacharan Mahesh only added to that cocktail. Gossip flew around freely and various rumours were doing the rounds. People were talking about what might happen in the coming days and gossips about 'Devi' had already spread like wildfire. Everybody formed their own theories about the identity of Devi. The rumours ranged from religious fringes to the extent of some brand new superhero, who was speculated to have arrived to purge the city of Kolkata from evil.

Chauhan slammed the newspaper on his table in frustration. The rise of criminal activities over the last few days had become unimaginable. Jai entered his chamber and rushed towards him. He took out the phone he had picked up, opened the gallery and showed the pictures and the videos to the Commissioner. The two men scrutinized the content and then Jai sat on a chair opposite to his senior.

Chauhan said, 'This is a very crucial source of evidence, Jai. Well done! It will be a great help in our investigation. Do you recognize the man who is speaking with Akhilesh Ganguly?

Devi

He is Retired Major Digvijay Talwar. He is a famous person in Kolkata's social circles. There is an article about him in today's newspaper, too. Here, take this and read aloud.'

Jai took the newspaper and read the article that Commissioner Chauhan had pointed out: 'Retired Major Digvijay Talwar is a name that this city is not unfamiliar with. Even though he is a media-shy person, his work has reached far and wide amid the city's social circle. Ten years ago, after his retirement from the army, Major Talwar founded the Pride Institute–Orphanage Home in the suburbs of Kolkata. Today, it houses about three hundred kids. On the auspicious occasion of Maha Shashti, the children of Pride Institute–Orphanage Home would perform a cultural event at the Nazrul Mancha Stadium in Kolkata. Eminent personnel from the political and social strata would grace the event with their presence. Major Talwar would be felicitated at the event by the honourable Education Minister of State during the cultural ceremony.'

Jai finished reading and asked, 'I don't understand anything. What is the meaning of these pictures and videos, and how is Major Talwar connected to everything? He seems to be a respectable person!'

'The only person who can provide the answer is Major Talwar himself!' Chauhan replied adding, 'Jai, I want you and Arun to find Major Talwar and speak with him. Thereafter, you can resume your work on the Durgacharan security case. Hand over the details to Arun, so that he can investigate further. Meanwhile, I will visit Alipore and meet Durgacharan and ensure everything is fine. I have to pay a visit to the Spanish delegates, too. Keep me informed.'

Just as their conversation was ending, Arun entered the room. Jai briefed him about the discussion he had had with the Commissioner and what instructions they had to follow. Jai showed him the photographs and the videos as well.

Arun jumped with excitement and said, 'Jai, don't you recognize that man dressed like a gypsy? He is Samuel Gomes, the notorious drug peddler. We had been searching for him frantically a few years ago when he went undercover. Till date, we haven't been able to trace him. And now, he reappears in these pictures and videos!'

Arun took out the note that Savitri had received and read it again, 'Bhavani Shankha is in danger. The pagans are many. One is dead, but the threat remains. Devi will not let this happen. The evil blade must not auction the sacred conch shell…else mayhem will follow from her wrath!'

Arun continued, 'This note and the phone call that came from the anonymous caller are all connected. The mention of the recreational drugs directs us towards a drug peddler and these pictures show us Samuel Gomes! Isn't that an obvious clue?'

Jai was quiet for a while but he suddenly stood up in excitement, 'Sir… evil blade! This word has a meaning perhaps! In Hindi, *talwar* means blade! This note is directing our attention towards Major Talwar, I am sure of it.'

'That suggests Major Talwar and Samuel Gomes are somehow involved in a secret auction of the Bhavani Shankha!'

exclaimed Chauhan. 'Looking at the other photographs and the video recordings, I am sure Akhilesh and his brother Pranav are somehow related to this covert dealing and also with the murders at the Imperial Bank!'

The three men were elated with their discovery. Chauhan said, 'Arun, find Major Talwar. You need to interrogate him. Take him in your custody, but be polite with him, as we don't have an arrest warrant yet. Meanwhile, Jai, you go and spread your web. We have to catch Samuel Gomes. I will arrange for the warrants. Before the end of the day, we have to get the Ganguly brothers, Samuel Gomes and Major Talwar in our custody. I will visit Durgacharan to ensure everything is in order and meet the Spanish delegates, and then join the two of you here in my office by afternoon. The arrest warrants would be ready by noon.'

Arun said, 'Jai, my informers have given me some clues about the active drug smugglers in the city. I will hand them over to you. Perhaps that will help you track down Samuel Gomes.'

After a few more minutes of planning, Arun and Jai headed out, while Chauhan picked up the telephone to arrange for the warrants. He asked his secretary to get in touch with the court's magistrate for quick action. He knew this was his best chance to solve the series of crimes that had gripped the city during Durga Puja.

∞

Maha Shashti

Savitri had been sitting at her work desk and preparing for the day's schedule. First, she was supposed to complete a story about the ongoing series of crimes in the city and submit the same for online publication. Thereafter, she was supposed to visit the Nazrul Mancha Stadium to cover the cultural event by the Pride Institute–Orphanage Home. She was also supposed to interview Major Digvijay Talwar after his felicitation at the cultural event. This made her feel a bit uncomfortable. She had met Major Talwar previously at an event and had not liked his demeanour.

Presently, Arun called her on her mobile phone and updated her about his meeting with Commissioner Chauhan. Savitri exclaimed, 'I knew that the retired Major Talwar is a crooked guy! I never really liked his behaviour. I will be covering his event this afternoon. I shall try to get some information from him. Are you arresting him today?'

'Perhaps,' replied Arun. 'I shall confront him probably with an interrogation warrant and then try to get him to talk. I have been studying about him from my sources. This man seems like a deep-sea fish.'

'Come soon, Arun. I will wait for you at the venue. I hope this fog of mystery gets cleared soon,' Savitri said.

Arun disconnected the call and got inside a taxi. As the vehicle began to move, the cool breeze touched his face and his mind suddenly transported him to a memory... *Against a white misty backdrop, there she was, his beloved Radha. Her long hair fluttered in the wind and the sweet sound of her mischievous laughter rang in his ears, like music. The glow on Radha's face and the sparkle in her beautiful teeth, when she smiled, radiated a romantic luster to the frame. Arun saw himself holding her hands and laughing heartily. There was love in the air and Radha whispered sweet nothings in his ears. It was the time around Durga Puja. Everything was beautiful and perfect as he hugged her. Bells were ringing, drums were being played and it all felt surreal.*

The blaring honk of a bus passing by brought him back to reality. He realized that Radha was no longer with him. It was a day packed with upcoming uncertainties and perhaps more questions. Arun realized that he had dozed off and was now about to reach the gates of Nazrul Mancha Stadium within a few minutes.

∞

Chauhan asked the forensic department and the Cyber Crime Cell to extract all data from the mobile phone that Jai had found. He had been waiting eagerly to scrutinize everything in detail, especially the verbal communications and the locations where they were captured. The warrants for interrogation and arrest were getting prepared, and he was waiting eagerly. The warrants for Samuel Gomes were supposed to be handed over to Jai. Once these men were in police custody, all the interconnected web of crimes could potentially be solved.

Chauhan said to himself, *I need to act fast as soon as the magistrate signs the warrants. I must visit Durgacharan today and confront him indirectly. Let me see if I can extract any information from him.*

Jai spoke with some of the sources provided by Arun and also to his informers. The drug peddling circle in Kolkata was pretty deep-rooted and had its fangs dug profoundly into the various esteemed circles of the society. The elusive brokers were spread amid various strata, ranging from real estate builders to young students. Jai worked hard to gather as much information as possible. Using all his resources, within a short time, he was able to get significant knowledge from three most notorious drug peddlers in the city. He found out that Samuel Gomes was indeed in Kolkata and had been spotted in various parts of the city. The master of disguise, Samuel, had been on the run for the past few years and had vanished from the city. However, his recent reappearance proved that he had something to do with the recent incidents. However, Jai needed more concrete inputs to track down Samuel and get hold of him. He was certain that catching Samuel would help him solve the Bhavani Shankha case faster.

Finally, an informer, who was also a rival of Samuel, informed Jai over call, 'Samuel Gomes will be in front of Paria House at Park Circus. He will reach there at 6.30 in the evening for a covert dealing worth millions. Though I am not sure of the nature of the deal, I am sure it is something extremely precious that he is trying to smuggle. Be there in front of Paria House at 6.30 and you will be able to catch him.'

Jai questioned, 'How correct is this information? Are you

absolutely sure? Any misinformation can sabotage my mission.'

The informer replied confidently, 'Trust my words. I don't have much time. He will be there. Sir, be prepared with your best plan and you will receive your reward.'

Jai called two of his trusted aides and hatched a plan. He needed a backup but had to ensure that nobody knew who they were pursuing. He worked out a meticulous plan and discussed it with his subordinates. Finally, he called Commissioner Chauhan and disclosed the new information he had received from the informer.

The warrants were ready and the Commissioner gave his consent to Jai, adding, 'Collect the warrants from my office and also inform Arun to take the warrant for Major Talwar to take him into custody for interrogation.' Jai disconnected the call and then dialled Arun's contact number and asked him to collect the warrant for Talwar.

Arun replied briefly, 'I have already reached the venue. Please send a constable with the warrant to the Nazrul Mancha Stadium. Meanwhile, I shall wait here and ensure that Talwar doesn't leave. In the evening, I will meet you near the Paria House, if that is fine with you.'

'Okay. Sure brother.'

Arun met Savitri outside the gates of Nazrul Mancha Stadium. As soon as she met him, she said, 'Major Talwar already arrived quite a while ago. He is inside one of the private rooms on the first floor of the administrative block. The ceremony is about to begin in an hour. The delegates will start coming in a while. I think this is an apt time to meet him.'

Arun replied, 'No. I don't have the warrant yet. And I won't let you meet him alone. Let's wait for some more time. A constable will soon arrive with the warrant from the Commissioner's office. Stay here and keep a close watch, while I take a look around. We need to be very careful and not raise any eyebrows.'

Savitri stood and obeyed Arun's order as the latter walked away.

∞

Chauhan paid an hour-long visit to the Spanish delegates and discussed the plans for the next day. Everything had been set up. The Room No. 243 of the Kolkata High Court would be used as the interim courtroom. Representatives from the Indian government, the Spanish delegates, eminent police officers and lawyers would be present during the trial. A three-member panel of judges would review the charges, hear the confessions and allegations, and then announce their judgment at 11.00 a.m. Durgacharan would then be shifted to the location of his house arrest. The following day, Durgacharan would be shifted to Mumbai and then taken to the designated prison. Further hearing would be conducted post extradition. Chauhan briefed the delegates about the schedule and then left. He needed to visit the bungalow at Alipore where Durgacharan was being kept.

'Today, you will remain inside this bungalow. Tomorrow morning, the police team would take you for your trial,' Chauhan declared while sitting on the sofa in the living room. Durgacharan sat on another sofa, opposite the Commissioner and listened. Chauhan continued speaking in a low tone, 'Whatever I am asking is not part of your interrogation but for your own safety and benefit. Durgacharan, do you have a connection with Kolkata? I know your misdeeds are many but which of them associates you with this city? Tell me the truth and maybe I can save you from some unknown impending danger.'

Durgacharan laughed heartily and Chauhan cursed himself for asking the question. After calming down a bit, Durgacharan said, 'I am not a criminal. I am a businessman. I am related to every city in this country because of my business ventures. I am not involved in any criminal activity associated with this city. Moreover, your police department has been entrusted with the job of protecting me, how can anybody harm me? You don't need to save me from anything.'

Chauhan decided not to probe further or argue with the bully. He got up with a resigned expression and said, 'Very well then. Goodbye.'

As the Commissioner left, Durgacharan again had a hearty laugh and then slowly went back to his relaxed mood.

∞

At the Nazrul Mancha Stadium, Arun returned after fifteen minutes to the spot where Savitri was waiting. After another fifteen minutes, a constable arrived and handed over the warrant

Maha Shashti

to him. Arun looked at Savitri and said, 'Let's go inside now. I am all set to confront Major Talwar. Two of my men are here to assist us.'

The two of them went inside the Nazrul Mancha Stadium and headed straight towards the administrative block. They went up the staircase and asked one of the volunteers about Major Talwar's room. The man pointed towards the last room at the end of the long corridor and the duo hurried towards it.

As they reached the room, the door was unlocked from inside. Taking a deep breath, Arun pushed open the door. They could not hear any noise coming from the room and there was an eerie silence. Savitri and Arun quietly walked in.

Just as they entered the room, Savitri clutched Arun's sleeves tightly. She was in a complete state of shock. Her gaze were fixed at a direction and Arun followed it. In front of them was the lifeless body of Major Talwar on the floor, lying on his back. His left hand was close to his neck as if he had tried to prevent himself from choking. His lips had turned blue. His eyes were wide open and displayed a strange fear. In his right closed fist was a piece of paper and on the adjacent table, there was an empty glass. From the remnants of the drink inside it, it could be seen that he had just had a soft drink. Beside the glass was a small electronic gadget. Arun picked it up carefully and noted that it was a mini tape-recorder. He quickly called his men and soon the two constables arrived along with other security personnel. Within a few minutes, there was a huge commotion outside the room.

Arun carefully freed the piece of paper from Major Talwar's closed fist, secured the glass, so that it could be handed over to the forensic team, while some of the security personnel and the two constables carried the body. An ambulance had already been called to take the body to a nearby hospital. A doctor present at the venue did a quick examination of the body and declared Major Talwar dead. He added, 'This is a clear case of poisoning. I am sure that the forensic report will reveal further details.'

Arun unfolded the piece of paper. It had a few lines scribbled on it. He read the note: 'Devi knows everything. Only Devi knows what Talwar did in Baghmundi. His crime has been exposed today. He confessed to his crimes. The ghosts of Baghmundi are still alive to prove his crimes!'

And then he pressed the playback button on the mini tape-recorder. The recorded voice was that of Major Talwar who was confessing in front of somebody: 'I cannot face the shame. Baghmundi was the biggest crime of my life! I am sorry for everything. I don't have the holy conch shell with me. Akhilesh and Pranav employed me to negotiate its price, but I didn't steal it. They are getting good money for it. Only Samuel knows about the conch shell. I don't want to be a victim of Devi...'

Arun took in the gory scene in front of him before dialling Commissioner Chauhan's number and informing him about the murder. As soon as the latter picked up the call, Arun said, 'Sir, Major Talwar has been murdered. There are traces of poison in his drink. We have also retrieved a mini-tape recorder... Talwar confessed to his crimes. Perhaps, Major Talwar expected

Maha Shashti

to be spared by the assailant after confessing the truth. The poison was most likely sneaked into his drink before he was confronted by the assailant. Then, as he succumbed to the effect of the poison, the assailant carefully left behind the recorded confession, so that the police could get it. Sir, his confession clearly mentions the names of Samuel Gomes, Akhilesh Ganguly and Pranav Ganguly. It is a clear case of murder by poisoning. I am assuming that a lethal dose of poison, something like Strychnine, was mixed in his drink. We will get a clearer picture after we receive the forensic report.'

'Another high-profile murder?!' Chauhan exclaimed. 'Secure the place, and come and meet me at my office.'

Within the next forty minutes, Arun scrutinized the entire room thoroughly and searched every corner for any clue. The media personnel and the organizers had already gathered, as the news about the murder had spread like wildfire. The crowd outside the room had inflated manifold. Arun's subordinates had arranged for more police backup and the place had been secured. There was absolute chaos at the Nazrul Mancha Stadium. A police photographer clicked pictures of the scene and the body, and then the constables covered the body with a white shroud and took it away.

Arun looked at Savitri and said, 'Come, let's go. I will drop you at your office and head to meet the Commissioner at his. Things are looking very grim and I need to assist Jai in the mission to capture Samuel Gomes.'

Savitri spoke in a low voice, 'There are so many questions

about this tragedy. Why did Major Talwar get killed? What is Baghmundi and why is it his biggest crime?'

Arun stood beside Savitri and added, 'Moreover, how did Major Talwar know about Devi? Why does he fear her? What is the nexus between Akhilesh, Pranav and Samuel, and with whom was Major Talwar negotiating a deal?'

Savitri continued, 'There is more…who stole the Bhavani Shankha and how did it reach Samuel? Who killed the security guards inside the Imperial Bank?'

'Finally, who took those photographs and the videos and why did they give it to Jai?' Arun said trying to figure out everything.

'Oh God, these questions are so complicated!' exhaled Savitri.

Arun took out a pocket notebook and jotted down all the questions. After dropping Savitri, he reached the Commissioner's office and put forth his questions in front of Jai and Commissioner Chauhan, adding, 'There is another thing that comes to my mind. Poison is another attribute that connects the entire affair with Ma Durga. Snake is one of her weapons and most snakes are venomous. Once again, one of her weapons have been used to commit a murder. The connection is eerie. There are many intriguing questions that still remain unanswered. Who took the note and the poison to him? What is Baghmundi? What crime was Major Talwar involved in? There are many unanswered aspects.'

The two of them pondered for a while. Arun also handed

Maha Shashti

over the mini tape-recorder to Commissioner Chauhan and said, 'This is some solid evidence in this case and the other crimes, too, perhaps.'

Chauhan replied, 'I am sending Inspector Ram Manohar to arrest Akhilesh and Pranav. Meanwhile, you and Jai focus on arresting Samuel Gomes. If there is any truth to this voice recording, you should be able to recover the Bhavani Shankha.'

It was almost five in the evening by the time Jai and Arun walked out from Commissioner Chauhan's office. Meanwhile, Ram reached the gates of Ganguly Palace in Raja Bazaar along with three constables. He had the warrant with him. He looked at his watch and saw that it was twenty minutes past five in the evening. The Ganguly Palace was buzzing with activity, with the ongoing Durga Puja festivities.

Ram spoke with the gatekeeper sternly and then walked in with his men quickly. Akhilesh and Pranav were busy attending to their guests. The sudden arrival of police inside the Ganguly Palace created a buzz and a sense of confusion amid the guests.

The two brothers walked up to the police team with inquisitive faces. Ram was prepared for it. He took out the warrant and said confidently, 'Mr Akhilesh Ganguly and Mr Pranav Ganguly, you have to come with us. A warrant has been issued against you. You are being taken under police custody regarding several criminal incidents that have been taking place in the city recently, especially the theft of Bhavani Shankha. Please cooperate and come with us.'

Akhilesh sat down on the floor in a state of despair, while

Pranav said with a choked voice, 'We need to speak with our lawyers. You cannot arrest us just like that! We are honourable citizens.'

To this, the inspector added, 'Sir, this warrant gives us the power to take you into custody. You will be allowed to speak with your lawyers. Please come with us and cooperate. We don't want to create unnecessary drama here. I am saying this to help you save your own reputation!'

Akhilesh nodded in agreement and then the two brothers quietly walked out along with the policemen. The festive mood within the Ganguly Palace suddenly changed to one of anxiety and fear.

The two brothers were escorted to the police car parked outside the Ganguly Palace. Upon receiving the instruction from the Inspector, the driver headed towards the police headquarters.

∞

Sitting at her desk, Savitri wondered, *Why does the anonymous caller call Arun? How does this person manage to send messages to Commissioner Chauhan and Jai? What is the true identity of the Hijab-clad person in the Imperial Bank? How are all the crimes connected with Devi? Who is Devi?* She closed her eyes and thought.

Unable to find any answer, she decided to focus on writing her report on Major Talwar's murder case. She knew she had much more information than any other journalist. She wanted to make sure she did not divulge any such information that could compromise Arun's position and the work of the police department.

Meanwhile, the evening of Maha Shashti was full of grandeur. The entire city of Kolkata was shining with luminous decorations. Every street and corner was throbbing with activity and enthusiastic pedestrians flocked in front of the entries of the pandals. Every inch of the city was soaked in the festive mood. The recent spike in gory crimes had become a topic of hot discussion amid the people who waited in queues outside the pandals to get a glimpse of Ma Durga's idols. Television channels were agog with news about the increasing footfall in various high-profile pandals and also alternatively organized talk shows where commentators debated about the ongoing crimes. The overall atmosphere was that of high-octane drama.

∞

Around six in the evening, Jai, Arun and a team of two constables and two sub-inspectors reached in front of Paria House at Park Circus. The locality was somewhat secluded. The men parked their car in one of the side streets. Paria House was located on a road that was at a right-angle from the side street. This was done to make sure the car would not be visible to anybody. They needed to avoid any scope of suspicion. Arun suggested that he should stay around the vehicle. The two constables and two sub-inspectors took their positions at various points around the house. Jai, dressed like an ordinary guy, strolled casually along the street and kept an eye on the spot where Samuel was supposed to come. The dark veil of evening had descended and the dim streetlights cast long shadows of the big houses in the vicinity. In such darkness, the road in front of Paria House looked even more secluded.

Soon it was 6.30 p.m. and everyone became alert. Samuel Gomes could arrive any moment. There was anxiety and tension in the air. Would Samuel come there? Would the police team be able to nab him? Everything was unknown. Jai realized that there were beads of sweat on his forehead and he could feel his heart beating loudly. Time moved on and it was already ten minutes past 6.30. A sense of impatience was slowly gripping Jai. He felt uncomfortable and worried about what would happen next.

After another twelve minutes, a bicycle rider arrived in front of the Paria House. As the bicycle stopped, a man alighted from it casually and parked it against a lamp post. The man looked around and stood against the boundary wall of the Paria House. There was a small handbag that he clutched firmly and stood like an unsuspecting local fellow. Ten more minutes passed, but nothing happened. Jai winked at his team members and instructed them to wait. He had already identified Samuel Gomes, but wanted to see what he was up to. Jai was sure that Samuel was there to smuggle the Bhavani Shankha, and he wanted to also catch the person who might come to take it. This was a big opportunity.

Suddenly, a car came at the main road. Seeing the car,

Maha Shashti

Samuel suddenly dashed towards it with an attempt to throw the bag inside it. Jai understood the intention and pounced like a tiger. The two fell down on the footpath. Samuel had not been able to throw the bag and struggled to free himself. The two sub-inspectors chased the car, but it sped away. One of the constables noted down the registration number of the car while the other quickly reached to help Jai.

As the constables and the sub-inspectors arrived, Jai punched Samuel on his face and took the bag away from him. The other policemen overpowered Samuel as he growled like a wild cat in anger. Jai opened the handbag and out came a brilliant-looking, jewel-studded conch shell. Jai exclaimed, 'Bhavani Shankha!'

Samuel winced in pain as the policemen made him stand and handcuffed him. Jai slapped him thrice, before Samuel could even utter anything and said, 'Samuel, I am arresting you for the theft and intended smuggling of the famous Bhavani Shankha. You scoundrel! You cannot escape from the clutches of law. You have been hiding for a long time, but now your game is over.'

Samuel wanted to speak, but as he was about to say something, a soundless object whizzed through the air and struck him through the heart! In that moment of shock, Jai and the other policemen saw that it was a small but fatally sharp trident that had been thrown at Samuel with such precision that it had pierced through his heart. Before Jai and the others could figure out what was happening, Samuel screamed in pain. Jai took out his revolver and shot two rounds in the air. Arun came running, and on seeing what had happened, he took out his gun and fired four rounds in four different directions. By then, Samuel had fallen unconscious on the ground in a pool of his blood.

One of the constables ran and brought the car, while the others placed Samuel on the backseat and rushed to the nearby hospital. Arun and Jai, both bewildered by the turn of events, sat inside the car. As they reached the hospital, the doctors attended to Samuel urgently, only to declare after fifteen minutes that he had been brought in dead.

Jai punched the wooden bench on which he was sitting and blurted, 'Just as we were about to get hold of a person who could have shed some light on everything that has been happening lately, he got killed! Who is following out activities so closely? How could anybody know about today's mission? I feel helpless!'

Arun soothed him and said, 'Jai, my brother, don't panic. You did whatever could have been done. There will be more opportunities to solve this mystery. However, the best part is that you have succeeded to recover the Bhavani Shankha.'

Jai simply added, 'I don't know whether I should be happy or sad. Arun, the Bhavani Shankha has been recovered, but we have lost two significant pawns in this entire game. Both Talwar and Samuel are dead. We are still in the dark about the identity of Devi and we don't know what would happen next or when all of this would end. What is that missing link? How is everything connected? I don't see any light through the darkness.'

'We cannot change what has already happened,' replied

Arun. 'Let us go and meet the Commissioner. Let us hand over the Bhavani Shankha and update him about what just happened. Let us hope the situation works out in our favour soon.'

Jai clasped Arun's hands and said, 'Brother, I hope you are right! I hope we are able to solve this riddle that has gripped this city.'

Within the next one hour, Jai and Arun reached the police headquarters and informed Commissioner Chauhan about what had happened. Jai then handed over the Bhavani Shankha to the Commissioner.

As he placed the precious conch shell on his table, Commissioner Chauhan said, 'Boys, you have done a fantastic job in recovering the Bhavani Shankha. This is a big achievement. You have made the department proud.'

Chauhan looked at Jai and said, 'Jai, you have done your best. It is a pity that we could not save Samuel Gomes. However, this was an unforeseen incident and beyond our control. Let us focus on whatever we have at hand. Our team has Akhilesh and Pranav in custody. We can interrogate them and extract some information.'

Arun replied, 'Even I was unable to capture Talwar! But I am confident that we can still solve this case. I strongly believe that all these crimes are interconnected. Devi is that connection. If we identify this anonymous entity, then we can solve all the murder mysteries. I also believe that a sinister connection exists between Durgacharan Mahesh and everything that has lately been happening in the city. However, that elusive connection is making things more difficult for us.'

Chauhan returned a thoughtful nod, while Jai shook his head in agreement. After another few minutes of discussion, Chauhan called his secretary and said, 'Call the personnel at the Imperial Bank. Inform them that the Bhavani Shankha has been recovered. Inform rest of the Ganguly family as well.'

Patting on Jai's and Arun's shoulder, Chauhan said, 'This is the first success we have achieved in the last few days. Media is going to be seized by a frenzy covering this news.' He looked at Jai and added, 'A big task at our hand right now is the safe transit of Durgacharan Mahesh from Kolkata. Tomorrow is an important day. Let us assemble and go through the final plans.'

Arun came out from the police headquarters and called Savitri on her phone. He briefed her about what had happened in front of the Paria House, how the Bhavani Shankha had been recovered and how Samuel Gomes had been killed. Before cutting the call, he said, 'I am feeling very tired tonight. I am going home. I need to sleep a bit. You be careful and reach home safely.'

Savitri knew she would be late. The breaking news that she had just received from Arun was something that she needed to report. She sat down to write her story.

∞

At nine that night, an anonymous man sneaked into the garden of the bungalow at Alipore. Amid the heavy security, the shadowy

Maha Shashti

figure crept up a corner wall and hid behind the bushes. The unsuspecting security guards were milling around the place, while the figure waited for an opportune moment. About half an hour later, as the security personnel sat around a garden table, the man slowly tiptoed through the shadows and slipped inside the living room. He dodged the constable sitting on a chair and climbed up the staircase to reach the first floor.

Durgacharan was inside one of the bedrooms. He had just finished his dinner. Dressed in a designer night suit and reclined on his bed, the flamboyant Durgacharan was busy watching television. The cunning businessman was unperturbed about his upcoming trial the following day. He was confident that he would finally be able to escape the clutches of law.

Presently, a few kids started to burn firecrackers outside the bungalow. The policemen tried to hush them away, but the kids had lit a chain of crackers that began to burst in a sequence of noisy cracking sound.

The anonymous man rushed into Durgacharan's room and pounced on him. Durgacharan was completely unprepared for this. The man punched him in his face twice and took out a small knife. His face was covered with a mask to hide his identity.

The man spoke angrily, 'Durgacharan, your fate is sealed. Your punishment is decided. The Devi shall not spare you. You must die!'

The assailant dug the knife on one of Durgacharan's left arm and he winced. He cried while writhing in pain, 'Somebody save me! Don't kill me, please don't kill me! Police, help!'

The firecrackers had stopped bursting by then. The security personnel sitting downstairs heard the scream and rushed upstairs. The assailant heard their footsteps and quickly jumped down from the window. Before leaving, he said, 'I shall be back. Devi will take her revenge. Be prepared, Durgacharan Mahesh!'

Durgacharan was in a complete state of shock. He was bleeding from his left arm where the knife had pierced his skin. One of the police officers took out a first-aid kit and started dressing the wound. Durgacharan shuddered and said, 'Inform the Commissioner! I have been attacked. This place is not safe!'

The policemen searched every possible corner of the bungalow and even the roads outside. However, the assailant was nowhere to be found. One of the men called the Commissioner on his mobile phone and updated him about the entire episode. The Commissioner had just finished his meeting with Jai and the other officers for the next day's plan.

After hearing everything, Chauhan replied in a shocked tone, 'I am coming right away!'

He turned towards Jai and said, 'Something bad has happened! Somebody tried to murder Durgacharan!'

Jai was speechless. He gathered his wits within a few moments and then called up Arun. Chauhan asked Jai to tell Arun to rush down to the Alipore bungalow. As the three officers reached Alipore, they found Durgacharan sitting on the sofa in the living room. He was in complete distress and was shaking with fear. The policemen who were posted in the bungalow were left red-faced with shame. Even amid such high security, the anonymous assailant had managed to sneak inside and attack Durgacharan. Chauhan gave them a piece of his mind and ordered a thorough investigation of the mishap.

Jai and Arun took stock of the situation, while Chauhan spoke with Durgacharan, 'No need to panic. We are going to boost up the security.'

'No!' screamed Durgacharan. 'This place is not safe anymore! He might attack again! I am too terrified to stay here even for another minute! Who is this Devi? Why is she taking revenge on me?'

With raised eyebrows, Chauhan asked, 'Devi? Where did you hear that name from?'

Durgacharan related the entire episode in detail while Jai and Arun listened carefully. After Durgacharan finished, Jai called Commissioner Chauhan aside and said, 'Sir, this statement again proves the authenticity of Arun's assumptions. The Devi mystery has finally trickled down to Durgacharan Mahesh.'

Chauhan replied, 'Yes. So, there is indeed a strong link, even though the motive is unclear. However, Durgacharan seems unaware of this name. I believe he is not lying. His mental state is not such. Yet, the attack is real and there is a looming threat to his life.'

Arun intervened, 'Sir, even though Durgacharan might not accept it, this attack proves that he has some connection with this city of Kolkata. We must find out. I have a strong feeling that finding the root of this allegation against Durgacharan will lead us to solve these murders.'

Chauhan nodded in agreement and replied, 'Yes, we will. However, now we have greater tasks at hand. We must shift him from this place immediately. Jai, prepare your men to cover location number 3. We are shifting Durgacharan to the new location right away.'

'Yes, Sir. We can take him in your car and head straight to the apartment in Bangur Block. He can stay there tonight and tomorrow, before leaving the city on Ashtami,' Jai replied.

The arrangements were made and the cars whizzed out from the Alipore bungalow. Durgacharan was seated inside the car, along with Chauhan and Jai, while Arun sat in another escort van. The convoy of police vehicles speeded down the street with blaring sirens and then somewhere amid an empty road, the Commissioner's car and Arun's van quietly moved away from the rest of the police vehicles and headed towards the apartment in Bangur Block.

By 11.40 p.m., Durgacharan was shifted to the next location. The sprawling apartment in Bangur Block was spread across a single floor. Thirty policemen were employed inside and outside the place to ensure complete security.

Chauhan, Jai and Arun stood near the gate of the apartment complex and discussed. Chauhan said, 'Tomorrow we shall arrive a bit early here. Arun, you must go ahead and investigate the status of the recent crimes while we supervise the peaceful execution of the trial at the Kolkata High Court. After the hearing, we shall escort Durgacharan back to this apartment and then meet up at my office in the afternoon.'

Maha Shashti

Jai added, 'I shall remain here tonight, Sir; I will not go home. This case is getting really serious now. I don't want to keep any loose ends. I will personally ensure that no mishap happens tonight.'

Arun agreed, 'That is a good decision. I shall continue the investigations tomorrow and shall update the two of you in the afternoon. Hope nothing bad happens overnight.'

Chauhan and Arun went away, while Jai returned to the apartment. The stars twinkled in a clear cloudless sky. The question about Devi and her wrath haunted the officers. Only destiny knew what was coming next while the mortals awaited their fate.

Maha Shaptami

An early morning flight from Singapore arrived at the Kolkata Airport at six. Among the passengers was an elderly woman of Indian origin in her mid-fifties. She cleared the immigration formalities and came out of the airport. She boarded the white sedan that had been waiting outside the exit gate. The chauffeur-driven vehicle zoomed down the road and, within the next thirty minutes, arrived at the Glistering Heights Apartments at Lansdowne Road. The woman entered the building and went straight to the posh apartment unit on the tenth floor. Outside the door, the nameplate read 'Ms Anita Gorai'.

Anita Gorai was aging, but every aspect of her personal grooming, beginning from the expensive saree she flaunted to the costly makeup she wore, reflected her upper-class stature and her refined sense of style. She was somewhat exhausted after the journey and freshened up a bit. She was the lone occupant of the apartment but had paid a hefty sum to a professional firm for its maintenance to ensure that everything remained perfect. Anita made herself a cup of coffee and sat down on the leather-upholstered sofa. She took out her mobile phone and made a call.

'When is the trial supposed to begin? I am here in Kolkata,' asked Anita while sipping her coffee.

'It will begin sharp at 10.30!' the voice from the other end responded.

'Alright. I will be there,' Anita replied and disconnected the phone.

As she finished her coffee, she got up from the sofa and went towards the bedroom. However, her footsteps halted in place as she saw a man standing right in front of her. The tall figure was clad in a blue-coloured hoodie and he held his gloved hands behind.

Anita exclaimed, 'You! What are you doing here? How did you come inside? I don't have anything to say…'

Even before Anita could finish her statement, the man swooshed forward and stabbed a sharp medium sized sword through her heart! Her voice faded and blood oozed from her wound. The sword had pierced her body with sheer force. The injury was fatal and the man pulled out the sword with equal force and brutality while Anita fell down on the floor with her eyes wide open. Her lifeless body lay in a pool of fresh blood and the man wrote the word 'Devi' on the floor with it. He exited through the window, climbing down the sewer pipe. He left the sword beside the lifeless body as a trophy of his crime.

Chauhan and Jai were all set for their big day ahead. They had to escort Durgacharan Mahesh to the Kolkata High Court premises where the interim trial would be conducted. Chauhan had already sent a team of officers to escort the Spanish officials to the venue.

Before leaving, Chauhan said, 'Jai, we have one more day at hand. It is well understood that Durgacharan's life is in danger. However, we do not know from where the threat is coming and that is what makes this case even more intriguing. Arun and his team are after the trail of the crimes that have taken place so far. You must join him after the proceeding at the High Court. I will ensure that Durgacharan is safely escorted back to the apartment.'

Chauhan was about to leave when the telephone on his desk rang. He picked up the phone and answered the call. However, as he spoke, the lines on his forehead became crunched together and his eyes expressed utter disbelief. He disconnected the call, looked at Jai with bewildered eyes and said, 'There has been another murder! The word "Devi" was found again at the crime scene!'

Jai returned a look of shock and replied, 'What? Who is the victim this time?'

Chauhan answered, 'A woman named Anita Gorai has been murdered in her apartment. The word "Devi" was written in blood beside the body.'

Chauhan phoned Arun and said, 'Arun, where are you? There has been another murder! Rush to the Glistering Heights Apartments at Lansdowne Road.' The Commissioner briefed Arun about the incident and added, 'The staff of the Molly Housekeepers entered the apartment unit around twenty minutes ago and found the woman lying in a pool of blood and the word "Devi" written beside her. Panic has spread among the residents of the place and the local police has secured the area. Arun, go there immediately and complete the initial investigation. Jai and I will be busy with the Durgacharan trial. Jai will join you as soon as possible.'

Arun replied after a pause, 'Sir, I received an SMS seconds before I got your call. Let me forward it to you. I will head straight to the crime scene.'

Chauhan disconnected the call and looked at the SMS he just received: `The Pagan may be dead, but the buyer is still alive. The Demon will escape lest justice is not meted out! Await the great escape and let Devi shower her wrath!'

Jai and Chauhan were quiet for a while and then the latter said, 'This message is like a riddle! We need time to understand the hidden meaning. However, first things first. Jai, let us complete our prime duty at hand. Come, we must ensure a peaceful culmination of the trial.'

The two officers got into their car and reached the apartment in Bangur Block. Durgacharan was waiting along with the officers posted for his security. A bullet-proof van had been arranged and Durgacharan was made to board the same. The convoy of cars, led by that of the Commissioner, sped towards the Kolkata High Court.

∞

Savitri sat on a wooden stool in front of the tea stall and looked at her watch. It was 9.13 in the morning. In front of her sat a man in his mid-sixties. He had a thin, emaciated body and a long face with sunburnt skin and untidy, unshaven beard. The man was Shahnawaz Khan, a retired police officer. Contable Ujjwal Roy sat with them and sipped tea from an earthen cup.

Savitri spoke, 'Mr Khan, Ujjwal dada told me that you had been on a covert case linked with Major Talwar. However, things went sideways…'

'And I lost my job and my honour!' interrupted Shahnawaz in a strong voice. He controlled his emotional turmoil and then continued a bit more calmly, 'Every time I think about that case, my blood starts to boil. The evil beings are roaming around freely while we, the so-called protectors of society, suffer the bruises of heinous allegations!'

Ujjwal added, 'Shahnawaz has been through tough times. However, with my persuasion, he has agreed to help us in this case.'

'I cannot change the past. However, I promise I will do my best to write about the injustices and try to bring out the truth. Please tell me everything about Major Talwar,' Savitri replied.

Shahnawaz smiled dryly and added, 'A few years ago I was a part of the team that was investigating a critical case. It was a secret operation that was being handled by a team under the supervision of ACP Hitesh Bakshi. Alas, the criminals got wind of our plans and killed ACP Bakshi. Then, they used political influence and pressure to dismantle the entire team! Most of the officers either made the supreme sacrifice or were arrested for various concocted allegations. I was lucky; I got the tag of a traitor and was suspended from duty. I am sure my murder must have also been planned, but I vanished from the city.'

Savitri questioned, 'What was this terrible case that took so many lives? Nothing appeared in the news media. The death of ACP Bakshi was reported as a suicide! I am shocked by this revelation. Please tell me more.'

Shahnawaz continued, 'A few years ago, a covert team of six men was assigned a special duty to uncover a scandalous crime. In the heart of the city of Kolkata, some high-profile people were involved in a ring of human organ trafficking. Many big names, including several hospitals, doctors and business tycoons, were involved in those deals. The stolen organs were smuggled via a covert network and were sold off for hefty sums. Retired Major Talwar was one of the men involved in this trade. The hideout for their operations was code-named Baghmundi…'

Savitri exclaimed hearing the words and murmured, 'Baghmundi! So everything has an association with Devi! This is such a complex affair!'

Shahnawaz continued, 'Our team raided the premises after receiving information that a secret transaction was to take place on a specific day and we had an opportunity to catch the culprits red-handed. However, our plans were foiled, as the gang was informed of the raid beforehand!'

Shahnawaz's eyes were red with anger and sorrow, 'They engaged in a fierce combat and foiled our operation! Some of

Devi

our men were killed and the remaining were threatened using political pressure! The killings were labeled as fake encounters and the entire episode was slyly covered up. The entire operation was presented as a futile one! ACP Bakshi had all the evidence, but he was silenced in his own house and the evidence was destroyed. His death was tagged as suicide and his family was threatened of dire consequences if they opened their mouths! Even though the operation was unsuccessful, the crimes at Baghmundi stopped abruptly. I heard that Major Talwar got scared and backed away. He was working on behalf of big businessmen like Durgacharan Mahesh and Vasudeva Patel. Major Talwar was their accomplice in many such illegal businesses, even though there is no evidence anymore. However, today, justice has been served! Major Talwar is dead and Durgacharan is behind bars!'

Savitri interrupted, 'Did you ever hear the name, Devi? This is really important. Durgacharan might escape his true punishment if we don't find out about Devi.'

'I have never heard of Devi,' replied Shahnawaz, 'Maybe it is somebody whom these criminals had wronged. I don't think I ever came across that name.' Shahnawaz pondered for a while and then added, 'There was something else related to the Baghmundi scandal. I cannot remember it now... I suffer from partial dementia.'

Savitri coaxed, 'Please try to remember. It will be really significant for the revelation of the truth. If you recall anything, please let me know!'

Ujjwal added, 'Let me call Arun sir and inform him about

this progress. Perhaps it will help him! I must ask for his guidance about our next steps.'

After Ujjwal called Arun and narrated everything he had just heard, Arun said to him, 'Tonight, you and Shahnawaz need to sneak inside the Police Quarantine Archives. I believe there are some files that Shahnawaz might be able to identify and those will help us discover a stronger link between Major Talwar and Durgacharan. If we get hold of something significant, it will help us uncover part of the story! The Quarantine Archives contain old and redundant documents that are subsequently destroyed. However, the process can be quite slow. If we can get hold of something that jogs Shahnawaz's memory about the case, we might be able to discover some unknown facts.'

Arun called up Savitri and briefed her about everything. 'Ujjwal and Shahnawaz will visit the Police Quarantine Archives tonight. This news must remain a secret, as we cannot trust anybody now. Let us see if we can recover something from Shahnawaz's memory!'

After disconnecting the call, Savitri said, 'I hope Shahnawaz remembers the missing links once he visits the Police Quarantine Archives. Everything has been truly mind-boggling!' She looked at Ujjwal and added, 'God knows what the two of you will discover tonight! Be careful. Thank you so much for helping us, Shahnawaz!'

'I consider this my duty, Ma'am,' Shahnawaz replied.

∞

The special courtroom inside the premises of the Kolkata High Court had a charged atmosphere. Chauhan and Jai escorted Durgacharan into the courtroom. He was made to sit at a designated position, while the Spanish authorities sat at a distance. The Indian officials were seated in their respective positions as the defence lawyer and the public-prosecutor discussed vital points. Chauhan and Jai took their seats too. The representatives of nationalized banks were present as well. It was a high-profile criminal case that involved multiple money laundering allegations against Durgacharan and his accomplices. The judges arrived and the trial commenced. The entire episode was supposed to be recorded via CCTV. The press and television media personnel eagerly waited outside the gates, awaiting the outcome.

Meanwhile, Maha Shaptami festivities were ongoing and the sounds of the drums filled the morning air. The proceedings of the busy day had begun from early morning itself. Before the crack of dawn, banana trees, immersed in sacred water and adorned in saris, like newlywed brides (*kola bou* or 'the banana tree bride'), had started to arrive at the pandals. This embodiment, also known as the '*nabapatrika*', gets placed next to the idol of Ganesha. However, there was also a sense of terror and uncertainty in the atmosphere, the source of which was the increasing crime rates in the city of late and the ongoing trial. A question echoed around every corner: who is Devi?

The prosecutors began their arguments and the proceedings continued with a high-octane dramatic atmosphere. Durgacharan's countenance displayed a perpetual virtuousness, as if he had done nothing. The arguments persisted for about an hour and the allegations were made and countered. However, nothing concrete emerged from the debate.

The defence lawyer claimed, 'The accusations against Durgacharan are under review. A few of these have been established, and the Honourable Justice will declare his verdict. However, under the present circumstance, most of the charges need further deliberation.'

The public prosecutor replied, 'Honourable Justice, even though many of the charges are yet to be ascertained, one thing is clear that Durgacharan Mahesh had defaulted payments to the nationalized banks and had been on the run for years. Considering the previous experiences and the present allegations, I would request the court to put him under strict house arrest and allow the investigating team to question him further.'

The discussion went on for another fifteen minutes and then the judges declared their verdict. The judgment was summarized by one of the judges, 'Durgacharan Mahesh will remain under strict custody inside a prison that meets with the Human Rights Agreement complying with the demands of the Spanish authorities. During his detention, he will be interrogated further regarding the open charges. Video footage of his imprisonment will be shared with the Spanish authorities to ascertain humane treatment of the accused. Durgacharan's imprisonment will be effective immediately and he will be moved to Mumbai tomorrow morning. Moreover, as part of the allegations that have already been proved, Durgacharan's personal bungalows and other properties will remain seized and be subsequently auctioned away by the government to pay-off the dues.'

After the verdict was declared, the courtroom trial was dismissed. Chauhan said softly, 'Many things remain unanswered. The outcome is still hazy.'

Jai replied, 'Yes, Sir. Many allegations will remain unsolved for years! Perhaps, Durgacharan will buyout political and legal indemnity and soon become a free man. Such is the power of money.'

'We don't have anything else within our power,' proclaimed Chauhan. 'Let us ensure that today and tonight passes away without much trouble. Tomorrow, this villain will fly away to Mumbai and I hope Kolkata will be spared from further ordeal.'

Chauhan stood up and added, 'Let me escort Durgacharan back to Bangur Block. You head straight to Lansdowne Road and meet Arun. We need to understand the reason why Anita Gorai was murdered. Perhaps, that will yield some more clues.'

∞

Akhilesh Ganguly and Pranav Ganguly were seated in a large room inside the police headquarters. The investigating officer, Niranjan Panja, had been quizzing them for the past five hours. The Ganguly brothers were on the verge of breaking down. The mental trauma and stress was beginning to deprive them of their energy. It was a distressing situation for the two. A lot was at stake and a lot could be lost. However, the interrogation had been relentless and there was no escape.

Akhilesh was the first to break down. He screamed, 'I will tell you the truth! I will confess everything. Just stop questioning us!'

Pranav added, 'Yes, we will confess everything, but we are not criminals!'

Inspector Ram Manohar, who was present along with Niranjan, started to record the confession of the Ganguly brothers on a tape recorder.

Akhilesh began, 'Pranav and I had been through choppy waters, financially. Our debts had been mounting higher and higher for two years and we were unable to stabilize the business. The Ganguly family has its heritage and social status, and it was becoming more and more difficult for us to manage the huge expenses.'

'It is then that we decided to sell off the Bhavani Shankha!' added Pranav. 'However, that was not easy. Bhavani Shankha has been a part of our family heritage for years! The 260-year-old conch shell is priceless. We decided to sell it off secretly and end our misery.'

'We got in touch with retired Major Talwar for negotiating a deal. He was a man with good contacts and was a perfect guy to approach for such a covert deal,' continued Akhilesh. 'He got us many customers, and one of them was Vasudeva Patel. However, none fetched the price we were seeking. At last, my friend Bikash Talukdar, former secretary to the chief minister, introduced us to Samuel Gomes, the notorious drug peddler.

We asked him to find a good customer for us.'

'Amid this uncertainty, something drastic happened! The Bhavani Shankha got stolen from the bank!' interrupted Pranav, 'We were scared! We feared a scandal and were devastated by the loss!'

'Then one day, Major Talwar met me at the club in Tollygunge,' added Akhilesh. 'He said that the Bhavani Shankha was in safe hands. He told me that he knew the guys and they are willing to pay a good sum to us. If we agree, then they would pay. However, the condition was that we would have to replace the original with a fake conch shell and close the police case. That way, the conch shell will reach the elusive buyer while the search for it will also end. No scandal, no apprehension. The perfect smuggling technique.'

'Yet, the price that was being offered was not as per our expectations. Akhilesh refused and they got angry! I convinced him to agree to the terms. The theft of Bhavani Shankha was a trick by the elusive buyer to put pressure on us to accept a reduced price and also agree to his terms of substituting the original with a fake one! We were apprehensive that if anyone ever found out about the fake conch shell, then we would face a greater scandal!' Pranav explained.

'However,' Akhilesh jumped in, 'considering our financial situation, we gave in to the pressure and agreed. Alas, before the deal could be closed, Talwar and Gomes got killed, and we are here in police custody! That night, Samuel was trying to hand over the fake conch shell to us, but someone killed him and the fake conch shell reached the police!'

'I hope the Bhavani Shankha is safe!' commented Pranav. 'We are facing the wrath of Ma Durga for conspiring. I pray we will be pardoned.'

'No!' screamed Akhilesh. 'The criminals have managed to keep it! The two biggest gems in that conch shell are priceless ones. Somebody is trying to mislead everyone. The Bhavani Shankha is still getting smuggled!'

The revelation took Inspector Ram Manohar and Niranjan Panja by surprise. They completed the interrogation and then headed straight towards the Commissioner's chamber. The news had to be revealed.

∞

Jai reached Glistering Heights Apartments. Arun was already present at the location and was investigating the crime scene in detail. Savitri had also dropped by. She needed to cover this latest crime. Police had secured the boundary of the apartment complex, so she had to take special permission to meet Arun.

Jai and Savitri stood at the crime scene, while Arun came up to them and explained the situation, 'This is another gruesome affair. The murder weapon is a medium-sized sword! It is yet another weapon that belongs to Ma Durga. The killer has written the word "Devi" on the floor with blood. The victim is Ms Anita Gorai, who lived on the tenth floor of the apartment. My preliminary investigation reveals that she had been living in Singapore for the last few years. She had returned to the city to renew her visa.'

Savitri took a closer look at the photographs of the victim and exclaimed, 'Arun, I think I have seen her before. I cannot remember properly, but I think she worked in the medical field. Can you do some background check?'

Jai commented, 'I have already arranged for that. Savitri, you are right. There must be something that associates her with the ongoing crimes. She must have had a past that we are not aware of. We need to dig deeper into it.'

Arun returned a worried look and said, 'First, a businessman, then a bureaucrat, then an ex-army man and now a lady with a secret background! This whole affair is becoming so puzzling. Amid all this confusion, we just cannot find the major missing link…who is Devi?'

As the ambulance took away the body and the forensic department completed their search, the police team sealed the apartment and closed the doors. Savitri took her leave and headed back to her office, while Jai and Arun got into the police car and headed towards the headquarters.

When the two men reached the Commissioner's office, Chauhan was listening to the recorded details of the Ganguly brother's interrogation. Jai and Arun sat down, and listened as well. The revelation struck them like lightning and the three of them looked at each other, surprise writ large on their faces. Everything was getting entangled turning the whole affair into a mess. The minor feeling of success after the recovery of Bhavani

Shankha—which had turned out to be fake—evaporated like ether. Chauhan banged his fist on the table and sat back helplessly. Officers Ram Manohar and Niranjan Panja left after completing their reporting.

Jai muttered, 'Do you observe an invisible link in this entire drama? Vasudeva was a potential dealmaker. Talwar was a covert broker. Samuel Gomes was a notorious smuggler. There was an elusive buyer who planned for an explosive step! Bhavani Shankha then got stolen and pressure was created to camouflage its theft. However, when the police became suspicious, every pawn was eliminated. Yet, the priceless conch shell has managed to reach its buyer most likely! The question is, who is this elusive buyer?'

Arun added, 'There are more things that are mysterious. Vasudeva was trying to buy indemnity for Durgacharan. Was this deal a part of that? Was the conch shell a compensation for it? Moreover, why were all these people killed? The police didn't know anything when Vasudeva or Talwar were murdered. Today, this woman, Anita Gorai, was also murdered. We don't know much about her involvement in the case either. We don't know why were all of them silenced and by whom?'

Chauhan commented, 'Finally, what role does Durgacharan play in all these crimes and why is the wrath of Devi upon him? If we are able to uncover the intention, it would help us link all the crimes that have been committed in the past few days. I fear what is coming next. Would we be able to ensure safe passage of the fugitive, along with the Spanish delegates, to Mumbai?'

Just then, Arun's mobile phone rang. Savitri spoke from the other end, 'Arun, I have found something interesting! Anita Gorai was formerly in the medical field. She was Matron Anita Gorai and had worked at various hospitals before relocating to Singapore. I did some digging and discussed with some of my veteran colleagues and informers, too. Anita Gorai had been a muse to many rich businessmen. Her association with these high-profile people helped her rise through the ranks and it is rumoured that her relocation was also funded by some of these men! She was perhaps here to witness the trial of Durgacharan Mahesh. I don't have any solid proof of this news, but I am sure it raises quite a few questions! Hope this helps.'

After disconnecting the phone, Arun related whatever he had heard from Savitri and then added, 'Anita Gorai was somehow related to this entire gory business. Yet, the reason of her murder remains unclear.'

Chauhan nodded his head and said, 'Good. Let us focus on finding the criminal and solving this intriguing case. I will ask my team to keep the Ganguly brothers under police custody for a few more days. This will ensure a dual purpose. It will ensure their safety and also help us dig out more information from them, if required.'

The time was well past noon. Arun got up from his seat and said to the Commissioner, 'I might go undercover. I will try to discover some hidden facts, something I might not be able to do if I remain on duty here. I will be too conspicuous. However, my camouflaged presence will not be doubted. I will not be available on calls, but I will remain in touch. Tomorrow, the two of you will be busy with the transit of Durgacharan. I shall use the rest of today and tomorrow to find out whatever I can.'

Presently, the telephone on Chauhan's desk rang and he placed the call on loudspeaker. A male voice from the other end spoke in an agitated tone, 'Commissioner Chauhan, I am Dr Amitava Guha. I am an anaesthetist by profession. There is something I must tell you and it needs to be discussed in front of Durgacharan Mahesh! I think I know who is creating this ruckus about Devi! I cannot say anything over the phone. I have just arrived in the city and I am really scared about this entire scenario!'

Chauhan quickly picked up the receiver and disconnected the loudspeaker. He replied, 'Dr Guha, where are you? We will pick you up from your location and then meet Durgacharan.'

After disconnecting the call, Chauhan said excitedly, 'Jai, we need to be quick. Dr Guha is in Hotel Aston Residency at Park Street. We must hurry and pick him up. This is the first time we have found a witness with a clue to this tricky problem. We have to be quick!'

Arun added, 'Sir, I will take your leave and proceed with my plans. Please let me know about any development in the case.'

Chauhan patted Arun on his shoulder and the latter made an exit. Accompanied with Jai, Chauhan quickly headed out. As they got into the police car, the latter instructed the driver, 'We have to reach Hotel Aston Regency as quickly as possible!'

Devi

The time was ten minutes past six in the evening and the festival revelries were mounting in the streets. Pedestrians were flocking the streets and the queues in front of the numerous pandals were getting longer. The Maha Shaptami celebrations were becoming louder with every passing minute and so was the traffic situation. Cars piled up on the busy roads and the traffic signals struggled to manage the overload. The Commissioner's car got stuck in the traffic and they had to wait helplessly amid the multitude. There was no shortcut available and the only way through was to wait patiently.

The usual twenty-minute drive took almost over an hour before they could make it to their destination. Jai rushed out from the car, reached the reception desk and asked, 'Which room is Dr Amitava Guha in?'

The woman at the reception returned a startled look and replied nervously, 'Room No. 403...'

Jai and Chauhan went up in the elevator and reached the fourth floor. As they arrived in front of Room No. 403, Jai rang the doorbell. However, no reply came from within. He rang the doorbell a few more times and knocked on the wooden door. Yet, there was no response. Chauhan's heartbeat was getting faster. He commanded, 'Jai, I think something is wrong! We need to break in!'

Jai called a few hotel staff and introduced themselves. Then with the help of a master-key from the housekeeping supervisor, the door was unlocked. Two of them dashed inside the room and then paused in shock! On the bed was Dr Amitava soaked in his own blood. Somebody had mercilessly cut his windpipe!

Chauhan regained control of his nerves within moments and screamed, 'Jai, call the ambulance immediately! He is still alive!'

As Jai and a few other hotel staff hurried outside to fetch help, Chauhan sat beside Dr Amitava, wrapped a towel around his neck to stop the bleeding and pleaded, 'Sir…who did this to you? Who is behind these crimes? Tell me…please tell me! We will save you, help is on the way!'

Dr Amitava was struggling for breath and writhing in pain. He muttered helplessly, 'Pa… pa… Paradise! Pin… Pink…'

'Sir, please try to tell me,' said Chauhan.

The futile effort didn't last long—Dr Amitava's breathing stopped and his body fell lifeless. Within the next ten minutes, Jai reached back to the hotel room and stood helplessly. The shocking news had already reached quite a few occupants of the hotel and panic was building up. Police reinforcement team did their best to control the commotion. The ambulance arrived within the next twelve minutes and the body was carried away. The supervising doctor checked him before leaving, sighed and told the Commissioner, 'I am sorry. He is no more. The injury was fatal and the blood loss was severe.'

As the room was cleared, Jai and Chauhan stayed back with two more police officers for a while. Jai searched the room frantically for clues. One of the assisting officers scrutinized Dr Amitava's belongings while the other inquired at the reception desk and analysed the CCTV footage. Jai ordered a quick interrogation of the guests residing on the same floor. However, after a thorough inspection that lasted two hours, they could find only a few details.

Jai summarized the points and briefed Commissioner Chauhan, 'Dr Amitava Guha arrived from Bangalore this morning. He hailed from Kolkata but had relocated to Bangalore three years ago. Today, a person came to enquire about him around 6.30 in the evening. The CCTV footage shows a turban-clad, bearded man enter the corridor leading to Dr Amitava's room. We have asked all the guests, but no one had met this person. It is obvious that this guy came to meet Dr Amitava. He is the murderer. The CCTV footage shows him leave via the same corridor, just moments before we arrived! The man deliberately kept his face positioned in a manner such that he wouldn't be captured in the footage. It seems he knew how CCTV coverage works, else he would not have been able to camouflage his identity so well.'

'Another crime has been committed!' shouted Chauhan, 'And we stand here helplessly! This is frustrating! Our only hope is also lost.'

As they left, Jai asked the presiding officer to secure the room and seal the place. They avoided the questions of the media personnel who were already mobbing the hotel lobby. Chauhan and Jai got into their car and headed back to the police headquarters.

Chauhan whispered to him, 'Jai, there must be a mole amongst us! Every bit of information is passing onto our elusive suspect! The criminal has access to the police headquarters. If only we could extract a motive and understand the modus operandi, we could have solved the case by now.'

'Sir, can we use Durgacharan as a bait?' asked Jai in a low voice.

'No Jai, that is too risky! Moreover, he will be leaving tomorrow. I hope we don't face more trouble. The CBI has already warned me after the first attack on Durgacharan. We need to be very careful,' replied Chauhan. 'I wonder what Dr Amitava meant by his last few words. He could utter two words, "paradise" and "pink". I couldn't understand what he was trying to say!'

Jai's phone starting ringing and he received the call. Arun spoke from the other end, 'Jai, I just received a call from my anonymous caller again! I managed to record it. I am sending it you. Listen to it. I didn't understand what it meant. He was speaking about Dr Amitava. I don't know what I am supposed to do with the message...'

Jai interrupted and explained to Arun about what had transpired. He added, 'I believe, now you understand how Dr Amitava features in the message from your anonymous caller. Where are you?'

Arun replied, 'I don't want to disclose my location over this call. It might be traced. Goodbye, I will return soon.'

As the phone call disconnected, Jai's phone beeped with the notification of the recorded call from Arun.

Jai played the message while Chauhan and he listened carefully: 'Dr Amitava is no sage! Check his records. He had been involved in several illegal medical cases in Kolkata. Alas, all of them were covered up with money! Now, the wrath of Devi consumes him! Doomsday is arriving fast! The Holy Conch must not strengthen the Unholy Legion!'

Chauhan and Jai looked at each other after listening to the recorded message. Finally, after a while, Chauhan said, 'Jai, I want you to be on guard at the Bangur Block. We must ensure complete security for Durgacharan. I cannot trust anybody else!'

Jai replied, 'Yes Sir! After reaching the headquarters, I will take a few of my best men and head straight to the Bangur Block.'

A few more minutes later, when they reached the police headquarters, Chauhan sat in his office and said to Jai, 'Tomorrow morning at nine, a special CBI vehicle will take Durgacharan from the Bangur Block. From that moment onwards, the cases would be formally handed over to the CBI. They will also escort the Spanish delegates to the airport. A high security flight will then take them to Mumbai. Till that time, we will have to ensure foolproof security! After that, we will return to this Devi case. By then, I hope Arun comes back with some good news…'

Jai nodded in agreement and said before leaving, 'Sir, I assure you, we will solve this case and also make sure that Durgacharan leaves Kolkata unharmed. We will not let you down!'

After Jai left, Chauhan sat back, closed his eyes and sighed, *I must think hard. There must be some clue, some loose end that would be a ray of light in this dark mystery!*

∞

Maha Shaptami

At around ten at night, Ujjwal and Shahnawaz arrived at the Police Quarantine Archives. The empty road inside the inner quarters of Topsia Colony was devoid of any human activity at that hour. It was in the dingy quarters of the industrial belt in the city. The darkness of the night had engulfed most of the locality and the only source of light was the dim illumination from a few streetlights that were still functional. The building had only one security guard posted at the main gate. It was not a high-security location, as most of the archived documents kept inside the building were invariably considered redundant and useless.

Ujjwal whispered to Shahnawaz, 'I will go and engage the security guard in a chat. I know him. You take this opportunity and sneak in from the backdoor. Don't worry, there are no CCTV cameras inside this Quarantine Archive. Be quick but try to find as much as you can about Baghmundi. Once you are done, get out through the backdoor and go straight to the bus stop on the main road. Don't stop! After reaching the bus stop, give me a missed call and wait for me there. I will catch up with you and both of us will return together.'

Shahnawaz nodded in response and then vanished into the darkness. Ujjwal took a deep breath and went in front of the main entrance of the Police Quarantine Archives. He looked at the security depot and said smilingly, 'Hey, Bikash! Are you on duty here tonight? This is Constable Ujjwal Roy.'

A middle-aged, short man popped his head from within the depot with a sleepy face and said, 'Oh…Ujjwal dada. What are you doing here at this hour of the night?'

Ujjwal promptly replied, 'I was here a few blocks away at my cousin's house. Before going home, I thought I will drop by and see if you are here. It has been ages since we last met! I wanted to see you and chat a while before returning…'

'Great!' replied Bikash, 'I was getting bored. Come inside and we can sit together and chat!'

Ujjwal got inside the security depot and sat on a stool. Bikash sat on another and the two began talking. Meanwhile, Shahnawaz sneaked through the backdoor and entered the Police Quarantine Archives. He walked through the dark corridor and entered the large hall that contained loads of discarded documents. Shahnawaz looked around to ensure complete seclusion and then took out his mobile phone and turned on its flashlight. At first, he was bewildered by the sheer volume of files stacked in heaps within the iron cabinets spread across the huge room. His head began to spin, thinking about how to begin his search amid this colossal collection of redundant files. In his bewilderment, Shahnawaz thought of a plan. He began to study the pattern in which the documents were kept.

Shahnawaz said to himself, 'There must be a sequence in which these are arranged. I need to understand that pattern. Then I will be able to look for what I am searching. Otherwise, I will be lost in this ocean!' For fifteen minutes, he tried hard. The absence of proper light made his task even more difficult. At last, he found a pattern. He muttered to himself, 'The shelves are categorized on the basis of year and month and further divided alphabetically. The closest rack to the main entrance contains the most recent files. That means older files are kept farther away from this main door. If I have to look for Baghmundi, I must begin somewhere in the middle!'

Shahnawaz slowly made his way through the rows of cabinets and started to scrutinize the files. One by one, he patiently studied each and every file that seemed relevant and scanned through their contents. Beads of sweat trickled down his forehead while he worked hard to discover something significant. Finally, after about one-and-a-half hour of hard work, Shahnawaz stumbled upon a pile of files kept at the topmost rack of one of the cabinets. His patience was waning. However, scanning through the contents of the files, his eyes widened with excitement.

'Baghmundi!' he exclaimed. 'And this is the missing link that I had completely forgotten!'

Shahnawaz didn't waste further time. He didn't want to be caught. 'I don't have time to study these files in detail now! I must take them away and get out from here quickly! Ujjwal and I can look into them after reaching a safe place!'

Shahnawaz was ecstatic! He had discovered something very significant, something that could give vital information about Baghmundi. Shahnawaz took the files in his arms, exited through the backdoor and began walking. Momentarily, he felt as if he was being followed. He felt scared, stopped walking and looked back. He could see nobody, as everything was pitch-dark. He turned around and walked at a faster pace. After reaching the bus stop on the main road, Shahnawaz stopped and made a phone call to Ujjwal.

As his phone rang, Ujjwal understood the signal. He diverted his ongoing conversation with Bikash and ended it, 'It is almost midnight! My wife is calling me home. I must leave now. Bikash, it was nice meeting you after such a long time!'

Ujjwal didn't waste further time and reached the bus stop. On seeing Shahnawaz and his smiling face, Ujjwal asked, 'Was the mission successful? Did you find anything?'

'Yes!' Shahnawaz replied, 'I managed to retrieve the secret Baghmundi files! I stole them from the Quarantine Archives. This has all the missing links and the cover-ups that were done! It will definitely help you with the investigation!'

'Let us go back to my house,' replied Ujjwal, 'We will study the files there. My wife is not at home, and we will have privacy. I will let Arun sir know about our success.'

The two men hired a taxi and headed towards the Police Housing Quarters at Kasbah township. Ujjwal lived there in a one-bedroom apartment. He sent an SMS to Arun and informed him about their plans to study the files after reaching home.

Ujjwal and Shahnawaz reached Ujjwal's first-floor apartment around 1.30 a.m. Amid the silence of the night, the two of them entered the house and locked the door. Shahnawaz sat on the sofa and kept the files on the table.

Ujjwal asked, 'Would you like to have some tea?'

Shahnawaz replied, 'Absolutely! I am very exhausted after

this secret exercise. I need to calm down. A cup of tea will be really rejuvenating!'

Ujjwal went inside the kitchen and turned on the gas. He lighted the flame and started to prepare tea. Within a few minutes, his phone rang and Ujjwal picked up the call. Arun spoke from the other end excitedly, 'I got your message! Are you alone?'

'No Sir,' replied Ujjwal, 'I am at home with Shahnawaz!'

'Quickly come outside, to some secluded place,' asked Arun. 'There is something you must know and Shahnawaz must not overhear it!'

Ujjwal followed orders and walked out from the apartment into the open corridor. As he was quite a distance away, Ujjwal said, 'Yes Sir. I am outside…please tell me.'

'I have discovered that Shahnawaz Khan was among the few officers who had betrayed ACP Hitesh Bakshi. Be careful with him! Take the files from him and make him leave quickly from there! Take those files to Commissioner Chauhan and tell him everything…'

Before Arun could finish talking and before Ujjwal could react, there was an explosion in his apartment! The gas cylinder exploded and the severity of the explosion flung Ujjwal from the corridor balcony onto the adjacent road. He landed on his head and immediately became unconscious as his spine cracked. Ujjwal's apartment was blazing with fire and the impact of the explosion tore apart Shahnawaz's body—he died instantaneously. Everything within the apartment was burnt to ashes. People ran around in panic and the fire brigade was called immediately. Amid this ghastly affair, the Baghmundi files too were burnt to ashes and their secrets lost forever! A few policemen picked up Ujjwal and placed him inside an ambulance. He was in a critical state. He was bleeding from his head and nose, and his neck was in a terrible state. He needed to receive emergency treatment, else he could have succumbed to his injuries.

Savitri was sleeping and got up hurriedly after getting a call from Arun late in the night. She could hear him talking in an anxious tone: 'Savitri... something disastrous happened to Ujjwal! Hurry, go to his home. Shahnawaz and he had found some significant files related to Baghmundi at the Quarantine Archives! I was speaking with him about it over the phone when I heard a loud explosion and his phone got disconnected. I have not been able to reach him since then! Commissioner Chauhan and Jai don't know about our secret operation at the Police Quarantine Archives. However, I smell sabotage again! Quickly reach out to Ujjwal...I fear that he is in dire danger! If needed, contact Jai and tell him about our covert operation.'

'Where are you? When are you coming back?' asked a concerned Savitri.

'I cannot tell you anything now! I am at a secret place. I will be back soon! Now hurry...' replied Arun.

Savitri didn't probe further and quickly dressed up and went out. She hired a taxi and headed towards the Police Housing Quarters at Kasbah township. It was early in the morning now, and it took Savitri around twenty minutes to reach. As she entered the housing complex, she was astonished looking at the horrifying sight. The fire brigade had fought hard to bring the fire under control. People were panicking and many policemen were running around to ensure safety of the other families living in the area.

Savitri got hold of one of the officers and asked, 'Sir, what happened here? Have you seen Mr Ujjwal Roy? I am his friend.'

The officer replied in a state of shock, 'The gas cylinder inside Ujjwal Roy's apartment exploded. He was standing in the balcony corridor and was flung down onto the road due to the impact. He is being taken to the Police Hospital, as he is in a critical condition! There was another person inside his apartment, but he was burnt alive! We don't know about his identity yet.'

Savitri was left speechless! She sat down on a bench and started to weep. She said to herself, 'Oh God! What a horrific affair! Shahnawaz Khan got burnt alive and the Baghmundi files are most likely lost forever! Ujjwal dada is in a critical state. Arun is undercover! What am I going to do? I cannot understand anything…'

Savitri wept for a while and then made a phone call to Jai. He was already aware of the accident and listened to Savitri. She hurriedly explained, 'Constable Ujjwal Roy is in a critical state! Arun is in hiding and I didn't know whom to contact, so I called you! Ujjwal dada had unearthed some vital information about Baghmundi as per Arun's instructions. Alas, it is all lost!'

Jai replied, 'Wait at the Kasbah township. I will reach there shortly. We can go and meet Commissioner Chauhan thereafter. What was Arun trying to discover about Baghmundi? We need to know everything. Only then can we fix the ongoing crisis!'

Savitri disconnected the phone and sat down quietly amid that pandemonium. Dawn was slowly approaching the doorsteps of the dark night and a new morning was waiting to unveil itself soon.

Maha Ashthami

Jai and Savitri reached Chauhan's office at seven in the morning. He had already arrived an hour earlier and was busy with the preparations for the big day. Savitri sat on a chair in front of him and revealed the entire episode of meeting Shahnawaz Khan and Ujjwal Roy, and their subsequent plans to visit the Police Quarantine Archives to dig out further classified information. Chauhan expressed his discomfort on not being aware of the entire plan.

Savitri exclaimed, 'Sir, Arun wanted to ensure complete secrecy due to the fragile nature of the situation and thus refrained from disclosing the plans to you.'

Chauhan replied, 'Savitri, I don't like to remain in the dark! Had Arun told us about his plans, perhaps we could have ensured greater security! Moreover, he involved Shahnawaz Khan, a person who is no longer in active police duty! This is something that needed my intervention! However, the damage has already been done and we can only look forward to the future now.'

Jai responded, 'Sir, the Baghmundi affair seems to have some significance in our present scenario. Maybe we should probe it further. It might help us discover unknown facts and lead us to solve the mystery of Devi!'

Savitri commented, 'Sir, I will do my own research and look in the archives of the *Kolkata Chronicle*. I will also talk to some senior journalists and try to find out something relevant.'

Jai replied, 'Savitri, I will meet you at your office today before noon. Before that, Commissioner Chauhan and I will be busy with the transit of Durgacharan. As soon as we complete this task, I will give you a call and meet you. We don't know when Arun will return, but we must do our best to uncover any hidden truth!'

After Savitri left, Chauhan commented, 'Jai, soon the special vehicle from the CBI will be at the Bangur Block apartment. Let us hurry down to the location and ensure that everything works as per our plans. The airport is not far from Bangur Block and I hope the handover of the fugitive will be a peaceful one. The Home Ministry is pretty worried about the ongoing crisis.'

In the next forty minutes, Chauhan and Jai reached the Bangur Block apartment complex. A tight police security had been arranged to warrant full protection. The special CBI vehicle was parked at the entrance and three armed officers were busy taking handover of the relevant documents. At 9.30 a.m, Chauhan completed all the handover formalities while Jai escorted Durgacharan from the apartment. The entire operation was being done in complete secrecy to avoid any further calamity.

Durgacharan looked at Chauhan and said with a smirk, 'You have taken good care of me. I can forgive the little incident that took place at our previous hideout. If you ever need a favour, just remember me. I always repay my debts.'

Chauhan replied with repugnance, 'I hope I never need a favour from you, Durgacharan. Think about all your misdeeds. Much has happened ever since you arrived in our city. I wonder how you camouflage your true colours.'

'I am completely innocent!' replied Durgacharan. 'The little problems with my loans will soon vanish and I will be a free man again.'

Durgacharan quickly got inside the special CBI vehicle, along with the two escorting officers. The other two officers sat in the front seats. The car left the apartment complex and zoomed away.

Jai commented, 'They will go via the Rajarhat bypass connector. As per the instructions from the CBI, we have deliberately refrained from using escort vehicles to avoid unnecessary alarm. Rajarhat bypass will be the fastest route today. I have asked the traffic department to keep all traffic away from that road, so that the CBI vehicle can swiftly pass through. This will also serve a dual purpose of evading our elusive enemy and stopping him from knowing how and when we would be transferring Durgacharan. A police patrol team will meet them at the end of the bypass and lead them to the airport. The Spanish authorities will also reach the airport in a special vehicle and meet the CBI officials directly there. I really hope that this arrangement proves to be foolproof.'

Chauhan replied, 'I hope so too! Let me now go back to my office. I need to sit and think hard. I need to put together the fragments and draw the complete picture. Jai, go and meet Savitri at her office and see if you can find anything relevant. I hope Arun returns soon.'

∞

Savitri reached her office directly after visiting the Commissioner. Then she searched the archives of the *Kolkata Chronicle* frantically, yet patiently, with the hope of finding something useful. She managed to sneak into the office building at an early hour and then bribed the security guard to let her inside the room where old archives had been kept. She worked relentlessly for almost two hours while her nerves remained charged with suspense and mystery. Finally, her patience paid off and she could find a copy of an unpublished report by an independent journalist. The title of the report read, 'Codename Baghmundi Scandal'. Savitri grabbed the pile of papers and quickly slipped away inside her cabin.

'Mother Luck is with me today!' she smiled to herself. 'I hope Maha Ashthami brings good luck and fortune to us!'

Savitri sat in her cabin and studied the report closely. The more she read, the more bewildered she felt. She took out her pocket diary and jotted down significant points from the report. Her phone rang and at that moment she realized that it was almost 10.10 in the morning.

Maha Ashthami

As she answered the phone, Jai spoke from the other end, 'I am standing below your office. Can you come down?'

Savitri took the papers and quickly went to the entrance of the office building. After meeting Jai, the two of them went inside a nearby coffee shop and sat down. Savitri's eyes reflected a thrill that Jai could read easily.

Savitri showed the unpublished report to Jai and said, 'This is a three-year-old report by an independent correspondent. I don't know who the reporter was. The report does not mention any name. I guess the person deliberately refrained from mentioning it. However, this report was never printed for obvious reasons. It contains startling information about the Baghmundi case! However, proving these claims was a big challenge and that is why, maybe, the report didn't see the light of day.'

Jai scanned through the document while Savitri spoke, 'Look, the report states the involvement of Durgacharan Mahesh and Major Talwar in the organ trafficking cases, and provides references to the manner in which the money was siphoned off by Durgacharan via Vasudeva Patel! Another startling point mentioned here is the association of Anita Gorai—she was involved with these two men in the heinous crimes! However, details of the crimes are not mentioned here. There are fragments of information that hint at criminal activities of doctors associated with hospitals and nursing homes! Nothing is written specifically. I don't know how exactly Durgacharan, Anita Gorai and Vasudeva were involved in those crimes. There are claims about big politicians who had received huge favours and monetary benefits in return for facilitating the crimes! Durgacharan has cleverly siphoned off money through numerous accounts. He himself made a fortune out of these illegal acts and then displayed a clean face in front of the entire world. I believe the editor of the *Kolkata Chronicle* decided not to print this explosive report without proper police verification…which unfortunately never happened.'

Jai was studying the report minutely. He added thoughtfully, 'Here, the report has specified the name of Retd Commissioner Mahadev Kanti. He was the commissioner of police before Commissioner Chauhan took charge. It also mentions that Commissioner Kanti was removed from his duty and was subsequently replaced due to a controversy involving the death of ACP Hitesh Bakshi. The report claims that it was all a part of a deep-rooted conspiracy! Medical scandals, illegal organ market, murder, deceit…what a concoction!'

Savitri looked at Jai and asked, 'Is it possible to meet Retd Commissioner Kanti? Do you know where he lives now? I think he will be able to shed some light on this case.'

'Well, I think I know where he used to live. However, I am not sure whether he still resides there,' responded Jai, 'Nonetheless, we can definitely drop by and check!'

'Let's go! It's our last chance to discover the unknown facts,' added Jai after a pause. 'If we are lucky, we might be able to gather significant intelligence to solve this intricate mystery!'

Savitri and Jai got up and quickly came out from the coffee

shop. Jai hired a taxi and directed the driver, 'Take us to Dover Lane, near Gariahat…'

Savitri looked at Jai and the latter said with a smile, 'He used to live in a bungalow at Dover Lane. We have to test our luck.'

Amid the ongoing festivities of Maha Ashthami, the taxi slowly progressed through the busy streets. On this day, Sandhi Puja is performed to worship Goddess Durga in her fierce form, the form she took when she slayed Chanda and Munda, the two accomplices of Mahisasura, in her battle to kill the demon. Worshippers and devotees line up near the mandap at nearly all puja pandals and offer the customary *anjali* (oblations). Being the most important of all days, there was a heavy rush of people and traffic. Savitri and Jai waited patiently inside the taxi as the driver manoeuvred through the roads and finally reached Dover Lane.

Jai asked the driver to stop the vehicle in front of a mid-sized bungalow. The inscription on the nameplate read, 'Kailash'.

Savitri noted, 'Kailash…the residence of Mahadev! I hope we are able to meet him.'

Jai and Savitri walked in through the open gate and reached the door. The bungalow was square-shaped and reflected an old English architecture. Jai commented, 'The house seems to have received a fresh coat of paint recently. At least, somebody still lives here. I am keeping my fingers crossed.'

Jai knocked on the door and a moderately tall, aged man opened it. The man had a round face with crumpled skin and white hair. He looked much older than his actual age and it was obvious that his health was failing.

Jai's eyes lit up on seeing the man; he saluted and said, 'Sir, I am Officer Jai Pradhan. I don't think you remember me. I have known you from the time when you were the commissioner.'

The old man greeted them inside and replied, 'I remember you, Jai. You were a bright and promising young man when I was still serving the police department. What brings you here today?'

'Baghmundi...' blurted out Savitri and looked straight into his eyes.

The three of them were inside the living room, and Savitri could clearly see the expression of alarm on his face. He asked Savitri and Jai to sit down on the sofa and questioned, 'And who are you, my dear lady?'

Savitri introduced herself and then Jai related the details of whatever had been taking place recently. He added, 'The case of this elusive Devi and the involvement of the Baghmundi case seem intricately connected. We are facing hurdle after hurdle in solving the crimes. Sir, we need your help...any inputs from you will be immensely useful for us.'

Kanti sighed and replied, 'The Baghmundi case was truly the biggest cover-up in police history! My entire career got ruined because of that. Big names, powerful politicians, major goons and heinous criminals...everything was a part of that gory recipe!' He paused and then added, 'When ACP Hitesh Bakshi was murdered, I could not tolerate the political pressure anymore and spoke up. There were threats to my family and I had to send them abroad. These people were much more powerful and removed all evidence related to Baghmundi and the murder of ACP Bakshi. I was scared and remained silent. They removed me from duty and I lost both my career and honour! The only thing that I could save was my and my family's lives...'

Kanti was in tears and spoke in an agitated manner, 'With the power of money, the criminals could evade the clutches of law! I knew Durgacharan was the mastermind behind everything but could not prove anything! Major Talwar was a mole inside the administrative machinery with deep connections amid the political and administrative realm. He was the guy who brokered all the deals and was a person whom I wanted to expose. Alas, nothing worked as planned and the truth remained buried. Young officers of the team were brutally killed and their deaths were camouflaged as accidents or failed encounters. Those who agreed to stay mute or switch sides were allowed to stay alive. However, their careers were devastated and their voices became irrelevant.'

'Is there anything else that might help us?' Jai asked eagerly.

Kanti thought for a while and said, 'ACP Hitesh Bakshi anticipated opposition and political pressure. So, he formulated a secret plan, which nobody knew about. He employed an officer anonymously, without anybody's knowledge, and gave him a few men...'

Savitri and Jai sat up with elevated interest while Mahadev spoke, 'No one knew who this secret agent was but it was a man from within the police department. This guy led an elusive team to continue the investigation parallely. This plan was successful and I was told that the secret team had collected significant knowledge and intelligence. However, after the murder of ACP Bakshi, everything went haywire and perhaps that elusive team, too, got lost! Yet, nobody ever came to know who those men were. Perhaps, they are still alive or perhaps they got killed…I don't know!'

'Sir, can you recall any name, any person who might have been a part of this secret team?' asked Jai. 'Maybe if we could get hold of one such person, we will be able to solve some of the mysteries!'

'I can only remember the name of one person…' replied Mahadev Kanti, 'He was a constable who warned me to protect myself after ACP Bakshi got murdered. His name was…Ujjwal Roy! I still remember him. However, I don't know whether he is still in the police force.'

Savitri was speechless. Her mind was in a whirlwind while she remained silent. *Ujjwal dada? What? He was aware of the Baghmundi case! So, why did he pretend in front of us? Why did he lead Shahnawaz to his death? What is going on?*

Jai was equally shocked but refrained from reacting. After the conversation, Kanti pleaded, 'I don't want to be dragged into this case… I am a failed officer and I cannot afford to risk my family. Keep me out from everything…it is an earnest request!'

Savitri and Jai got up to leave. Once they were out in the street, Jai said, 'Ujjwal Roy knows a lot of things that we still don't. I wonder whether Arun is aware of this! I am eagerly waiting for his return.'

Savitri replied, 'It's a pity that we cannot question Ujjwal dada now. He is in coma and nobody knows when he will regain consciousness…'

∞

In another part of the city, the CBI vehicle sped along the Rajarhat bypass connector. The traffic police had restricted car movement along the stretch until the CBI vehicle reached the airport. Durgacharan sat quietly in the backseat with his fists clasped and eyes closed. The journey went smooth and uninterrupted.

The car took a left turn along a crossing and moved into a straight road that led towards the end of the bypass. Within a few seconds, a large van appeared from a side lane at a high speed, veered in front of the CBI vehicle and rammed into it. The driver of the CBI vehicle pressed the brakes and the car came to a screeching halt! The large van stopped adjacent to the CBI vehicle and in a flash of a moment, three masked men jumped out from it. Durgacharan's head banged onto the roof of the car and he recoiled in pain and shock.

The four CBI officers recovered from the sudden jolt and jumped out from the car. However, the assaulters were quicker and attacked them before they could retaliate. The CBI officers were rendered powerless by the masked attackers. One of the assaulters suddenly sprayed a gaseous substance on their faces, making them unconscious.

Durgacharan was speechless and then cried in distress, 'Please don't kill me! Please don't hurt me! I will do whatever you say! I will give you a lot of money…'

One of the assaulters took out a gun and held it over Durgacharan's forehead and said mechanically, 'Money cannot buy you your life; silence perhaps can!'

Durgacharan became speechless and froze like a stone. Another assaulter sealed his mouth with an adhesive tape and covered his head with a sack. He tied Durgacharan's hands behind his body and led him inside their van. The third assaulter parked the CBI vehicle at a side and, with the help of another companion, lifted the unconscious officers and placed them on the backseat.

The job was done at a lightning speed and then the masked men quickly boarded their van and vanished along the side lane, holding Durgacharan captive. The Rajarhat connector bypass was a straight stretch that led to the airport, however there were a few side lanes that went into the interiors of the city and steered towards the outskirts. With restricted traffic flow, the incursion was perfect and nobody had a clue about what had happened. Even before the patrolling police car could discover the CBI vehicle, the mysterious masked assaulters had gone far beyond the limits of their reach.

When the patrolling officer reached the CBI vehicle, he was shocked to see the unconscious officers. Alarmed, he spoke on the wireless phone, 'Emergency! Emergency! A CBI vehicle has been found. Officers are lying unconscious inside the vehicle and Durgacharan Mahesh is nowhere to be seen! He has been abducted!'

Maha Ashthami

Chauhan was in his chamber when the news broke out. He had been working hard to put the disjoint pieces of the puzzle together to formulate a working theory for solving the ongoing crimes. On hearing about the news, he screamed with anger, 'How is this possible? Why was the patrol car not following the CBI vehicle? This is totally ridiculous! We have lost our credibility in front of the entire country! This is an international showdown!'

Chauhan was fuming with rage; he summoned all his deputies immediately and commanded, 'I want a thorough search right away! We cannot waste any time. Use every policeman, every informer and find out where Durgacharan has been taken! Seal all the roads that lead out from the city. The criminals are likely to try to flee the city. We must intercept them. We don't know what vehicle they have used for kidnapping, so we need to search every car that tries to leave the city! They have made us look like fools!'

As the deputies left, Chauhan dialled Arun's phone but found it unreachable. There was no response from Jai either. He felt frustrated and sat down in his chair. The thought of answering to the government authorities and the Spanish delegates made him feel sick.

Phone calls came in like arrows and he had to answer all. The Home Minister himself, the chief of the R&AW and the the CBI chief were furious at the security arrangements made by Chauhan.

The Home Minister even warned him, 'Chauhan, if this mishap is not rectified within a day or two, I will have to take serious steps against you and your team! This is a case of national honour and you will face the wrath of everyone! The Spanish authorities have accused us of negligence and I cannot blame them when the fault lies at our end. Find Durgacharan…I want him alive at any cost!'

Inspector General Anant Sridharan; Ranjan Mukherjee, the minister of home and hill affairs; and Anirudha Goswami, chief of CID, summoned Chauhan with demands for a proper answer.

Mukherjee went on to mention, 'Our political party is facing serious loss of faith in front of the entire nation! We will not tolerate this! Chauhan, either find out Durgacharan or else you and your team will be finished! The central government is sending their forces and they will begin to comb the city along with the CBI officials. Do whatever you have to do and make it quick!'

After a while, Jai called back. Chauhan picked up the phone and expressed his concerns, 'Jai, where are you? This is the worst! The abduction of Durgacharan is the last thing that should have happened! We have been left red-faced in front of the Spanish authorities and our entire country! All our careers, all our unimpeachable reputation will be ruined!'

Jai replied in shock, 'I just cannot imagine it, Sir. I will join you at your office as soon as possible. Sir, I will not leave a single stone unturned to find out Durgacharan. I have just made an astounding discovery. I will meet you and tell you everything!'

From Dover Lane, Jai rushed towards the police headquarters while Savitri headed back to her office. She was also shocked on hearing the news about Durgacharan's kidnapping. Before leaving, she said to Jai, 'I will look further into our archives and try to find out more information about Durgacharan. I hope we find a clue about this Devi affair. Be careful, Jai. Things are getting more sinister.'

As Jai reached the police headquarters, he found Chauhan in a hysterical state. Jai tried to calm him down and made him sit down for a while. He related everything that had happened at Mahadev Kanti's residence and then said, 'Sir, we need to think calmly. Your sharp intelligence and rational thinking are our best weapons! Only you can solve this case. Tell me what to do and I shall do it.'

Chauhan pondered over Jai's words and then said, 'Jai, my boy, I think you are right. Leave all the case files and all our findings here on my table. Let me think and connect the dots. Meanwhile, you go to the Wireless Control Room and try to find any clue regarding the abduction. Deploy all your informers and try to locate Durgacharan. Meet me here at my office in two hours.'

As Savitri reached her office, she received a phone call from Arun. Savitri blurted out everything that had happened and said, 'When are you returning? Please come fast! Commissioner Chauhan and Jai need you…we need you to be by our side!'

Arun replied, 'I will be in the city in two hours! Don't worry, everything will be fine. I will talk to Commissioner Chauhan and Jai over the phone. My secret mission was not useless. I have found out that Shahnawaz Khan was a rogue officer who had gone against ACP Bakshi. That is how he saved his own life!'

'Then what about Ujjwal dada?' asked Savitri anxiously.

'I don't know anything!' replied Arun, 'This is new information that has thrown me off. Anyway, let me return. I will meet you at your home around seven.'

Savitri looked at her watch. There was still time. She went inside the archive room and searched desperately for anything that could be of significance. The search lasted for almost an hour and then she was able to find a few files that caught her attention. She sneaked out the files and went inside her cabin. *These are all reports from an independent anonymous reporter. This is interesting. Looking at the pseudonym, 'Truth Seeker', it is obvious that it is the same person who had written about the Baghmundi case!* she said to herself.

Savitri scanned through the files and she was suddenly alarmed. *Somebody had been regularly reporting about the scandals of Durgacharan and his accomplices. However, the newspaper never published anything! These files are a huge source of information!*

As Savitri read the contents in the files, her mental state became bitter. She felt a strange sense of deception, anger and desolation that was beyond comprehension.

∞

Two hours passed and now Jai was starting to feel desolate. No positive news had arrived about the location of Durgacharan. The news media was abuzz and reporters were screaming foul play. A sense of panic had gripped the city on the most important day of Durga Puja. Policemen were everywhere and widespread search operations were being conducted. The traffic was going beyond control and a sense of hysteria was increasing by the second.

Inside his chamber, Chauhan was patiently studying all the case files and scribbling on the pages of his diary. The desperation was paramount and the ace officer needed to work hard to prove his mettle. Presently, Jai knocked on the door and entered the room. Chauhan asked him to lock the door and then take a seat.

Chauhan began to speak, 'Jai, I have been studying the case files and have been accessing the dark web for some information. It is a skill that I mastered many years ago. Today, I broke the administrative protocols and delved into it again! I found some data that is really significant. There are some points that I have summarized and I think we can delve into their meaning to find a way out...'

Jai looked at Commissioner Chauhan while the latter continued, 'We cannot find the hidden motive behind the Devi incidents. However, we know one ultimate goal of the elusive criminal: it is to seize Durgacharan Mahesh! Now that he has succeeded in capturing Durgacharan, he will try to take his next step.'

Jai asked, 'What is it that you are thinking?'

'Jai, this criminal does not want to simply kill Durgacharan!' added Chauhan. 'He could have done it much easily and without creating so many riddles! He wants to prove a point. He wants to make an example out of the justice meted out to Durgacharan! He wants to show the world…something.'

Jai waited patiently to understand what Commissioner Chauhan was saying, 'Devi is not just a name. It is a symbol. It is something that the assaulter wants to scream and tell the whole world about! He has punished many people in the course of the last few days and every murder or assault was upon somebody with a criminal background or association with Durgacharan! However, the criminal has not killed Durgacharan. At least we don't have any report about it yet. He is keeping Durgacharan alive for some reason. We have to exploit that motive!'

'What should we do now?' asked Jai.

Chauhan replied, 'We need to send out a secret message that we want him to do his task. However, this should remain only between you and me! Not even Arun should be aware about this. This plan must not be known to anyone outside this room.'

Saying this, Chauhan whispered something in Jai's ears. The secret plan was revealed.

Jai replied, 'Sir, your wish is my command! This is a drastic and audacious step. May we succeed!'

'We will,' Chauhan said adding, 'Now listen to this carefully. Look at whatever I studied before I came up with the plan.'

Jai stared with amazement while Chauhan spoke animatedly, 'Vasudeva Patel had been organizing thefts of extremely valuable artefacts in order to sell them to some international organization. Bhavani Shankha was one of them! Money had been flowing down through numerous fake bank accounts and was being gathered secretly. The question is why? The answer is…to bail out Durgacharan Mahesh! The money was most likely to flow out to senior judges and high-profile officials and political heavyweights to dismiss his crimes and help him become a free man! Now, the important point is, our elusive assailant was aware of this entire process and something more…something I have been unable to put my finger on!'

Jai returned a questioning look and Chauhan replied, 'Let Arun return. I believe he will have some more information to give us. Meanwhile, do what I have asked you to. Don't reveal anything to anybody. This is the only plan left with us… If we have to save the honour of our country, we have to take this drastic step!'

∞

The large van carrying Durgacharan and his abductors vanished amidst the busy traffic of Maha Ashthami and quickly became inconspicuous. It was impossible to spot the vehicle amid the heavy rush and the car smoothly drove through various roads and headed towards its destination. Contrary to Chauhan's expectations, the vehicle didn't move out from the city but went deeper inside the central core of the city.

After almost two hours, the van entered a congested road and went inside the premises of an abandoned factory. One of the men got down and opened the gate. Durgacharan's kidnappers had been able to transport him to their intended hideout without raising any suspicion. After taking him into one of the inner chambers of the dilapidated building, the driver of the van drove out from the factory's premises. The remaining masked men made Durgacharan sit down on a chair and tied him to it with hard nylon ropes. Durgacharan's eyes were blindfolded with a piece of black cloth. He was sweating heavily out of fear and was gasping for breath. Terror was writ large on his face.

Durgacharan spoke in a scared voice, 'What do you want from me? Please don't hurt me! I will do whatever you say!'

Unbeknownst to Durgacharan, a fourth masked person had arrived inside the closed quarters of the secluded room. This person came close to Durgacharan and whispered, 'Your screams will go unheard. You can shout loud, but nothing will happen!'

'What do you intend to do with me?' asked a terrified Durgacharan. Beads of sweat surfaced on his forehead due to the rising tension.

'Devi will do justice! She wants your confession!' replied the masked man.

'What confession? I don't have anything to confess…' added a confused Durgacharan.

'Think hard, you devil. You do have a lot to confess to Devi!' added the masked man.

∞

As Chauhan sat inside his chamber, red-faced with shame, his mobile phone rang. He responsed, 'Commissioner Chauhan speaking…'

A mechanical male voice replied from the other end, 'Don't try to trace Durgacharan. He is beyond your reach now. If you try to mess around, it will cost you the life of this prized fugitive and leave you and your entire department appear like fools in front of the entire world!'

'What do you want? What are your intentions?' asked Chauhan in a furious voice.

'Devi wants justice,' answered the mechanical voice, 'If you want Durgacharan to stay alive, wait for the right time! He will be handed over to you soon. If you do anything stupid, it will be harmful for everyone…'

The call got disconnected before Chauhan could say anything further. The fuming officer threw down the mobile phone on his table and sat with a worried face. He buried his face in his hands and muttered, 'Devi … Devi, I must uncover this secret fast!'

∞

It was well past seven. Savitri waited for Arun's phone call patiently. However, by the time it was nine, she decided to go home. Her office was partially open on Maha Ashthami and the empty corridors of the huge office building looked scarily abandoned. She gathered her files and her handbag and came out through the main gate. She was relieved to see the crowd of passersby. The festivities had peaked and the entire city of Kolkata was buzzing with activity. Savitri managed to hire a taxi and reached home after almost two hours. Throughout her ride through the busy streets, she tried to reach Arun on his mobile phone, but the calls failed to connect. She felt a sense of discomfort and was starting to feel worried about Arun's safety. Once she reached home, she freshened up a bit and tried to contact him again.

Around 11.30 p.m., her apartment's doorbell rang twice. Savitri peeped through the eyehole and then opened the door with a smile. Arun stepped inside. He seemed agitated.

Savitri closed the door and asked, 'Where were you? I was trying to reach you for such a long time! Your phone was not getting connected. I was so scared for you. What happened? You look so worried…'

Arun held Savitri's arms and said softly, 'Savitri, there is something that you must know. I want to show you something. It is very important and it is related to whatever has been happening over the last couple of days.'

'Alright. Tell me,' Savitri replied after taking a deep breath. There was something that she wanted to express, but she decided to remain silent.

'To know what I am trying to tell you,' commented Arun, 'you need to come along with me. There is something that you must see with your own eyes! Tonight is the night when it is the most opportune moment for unveiling what I have discovered. Will you come with me now?'

'Arun,' Savitri replied with a smile on her face and tears in her eyes, 'I will come with you anywhere. Just tell me.'

'Alright then, let's go right away,' said Arun.

Savitri added, 'Give me a moment. I will take a couple of things with me.'

Savitri went up to her work desk at home, picked up some papers from her files and placed then inside her handbag and came to Arun and said, 'Let's go. I am ready!'

The two went out of the apartment and then boarded a white sedan that was waiting outside. The driver started the vehicle and drove away slowly.

'Whose car is this? Where are we going?' asked Savitri.

'Don't ask anything now,' he said. 'All your questions will be answered soon.'

∞

Chauhan jumped up from his chair. His heart was pounding and there was a weird expression on his face—it was a concoction of ecstasy, fear, anger and anxiety. His eyes were wide open and the veteran officer said to himself, 'How could I forget it? This incident had completely slipped my mind!'

He drank some water and thought, *Yes…this was the information that had slipped into oblivion; it is the most important piece of the riddle! It was there in front of my eyes all the while and I was unable to see it. What a fool I had been! The answers were sitting right there and I was unable to see them.*

The time he had spent pondering over the riddle of Devi had brought back a memory that he had been trying to remember for long. At last, he had figured out an important piece of the puzzle.

Chauhan uttered excitedly, 'The answer lies in…Pink Paradise!'

Maha Navami

It was 1.20 a.m. The white sedan drove through the gates of a secluded bungalow in Angnara village in Hasnabad Tehsil. Located near the banks of river Ichamati, this place was far away from the humdrum of the festivities, isolated from unnecessary human intervention. Arun and Savitri got down from the car and he led her through the dimly lit muddy pathway reaching the main entrance of the bungalow. In the darkness and eerie silence of the night, the entire atmosphere carried a strange mysterious hue. Savitri's heart was palpitating. For the first time, she was feeling scared of Arun. There was something that was troubling her. Even in her moment of fear, she gathered her wits and secretly switched on the voice recorder of her mobile phone.

Arun knocked on the door and an elderly man opened it and let them inside. Arun said, 'Savitri, this is Bulaki Singh, the caretaker of this bungalow. This is an ancestral house belonging to my late grandfather.'

'Arun, why have we come here?' Savitri asked in a shaky voice. 'I am feeling scared.'

Arun smiled, held her hand softly and took her inside a room and said, 'Please sit down. Don't be afraid. You are completely safe here.'

As Savitri sat on the wooden sofa, Arun opened a drawer and took out a piece of paper. He walked up to Savitri and handed it to her. He stared at the questioning look on Savitri's face and said, 'Behold... Devi!'

With eyes wide open, Savitri saw that it was a picture of a little girl. Savitri froze as she stared at the photograph. There was a tinge of familiarity in the face of the girl and the photograph indicated that she was probably about two years old. Yet, her physical features seemed less defined compared to her age. Her smile had an innocence and an anomaly that made Savitri feel somewhat uncomfortable. The underdeveloped features, along with the innocent eyes of the child, reduced Savitri to tears. She was still unable to fathom what she had just heard... Arun had just mentioned Devi!

She now had numerous questions and she frantically tried figuring out the answers in her mind. She was utterly confused and struggled to understand what was happening. The threshold of her fear and terror had almost been breached. Savitri muttered in a soft and timid voice, 'What did you say? Arun, did you just say...Devi?'

Savitri sat motionless while a video began to play on the television. It was like a collage of life events captured in a tale, starting to unfold. Savitri shivered, feeling an intense anticipation while bracing herself for Arun's next words.

Tears began to roll down her eyes as she looked at Arun's eyes. He seemed to have no fear. All she could see was sadness. With startling clarity, she realized that the person whom she had loved unconditionally was the one behind the rampant crimes that had gripped her city! She was in a state of shock; this was something beyond her imagination. Savitri uttered, 'Why Arun? What is the meaning of all this? Why did you keep me in the dark?'

Arun sat on a chair opposite Savitri and began to speak, 'Savitri, you have every right to blame me. However, I urge you to listen to everything before coming to a conclusion. There are many things that you must know and only then will the entire picture make sense to you. Don't misunderstand me, Savitri. Will you please listen to everything I have to say?'

Savitri took a deep breath and spoke with a hardened jaw, 'Yes Arun. I will listen to you. I need to know how badly my trust and love had blinded me!'

Arun continued in a calm tone—his mind seemed to be floating amid distant memories. 'Devi is my daughter! She was born on the fateful night when Radha breathed her last! I have kept her hidden away from the eyes of this cruel world and now she lives the life of an orphan in a place where nobody can touch her! Her birth was supposed to be like the arrival of a gust of sweet breeze. However, she was brought into this cruel world with an underdeveloped mind and body. As if that was not enough torment, she also lost her mother. Her dementia makes her forget her memories. Sometimes, she even forgets me, her father!'

Arun paused momentarily, wiped his tears and drank some water. He looked at Savitri and began again, 'Three years ago, ACP Bakshi employed me in a secret mission to uncover the secrets of Baghmundi. He knew that there were looming threats on his core team and he wanted me to work on the case covertly. Under this mission, I conducted quite a few startling investigations and even engaged in unlawful practices to ensure my camouflage. Together with ACP Bakshi and his team, we were able to unearth mind-boggling intelligence about the human organ trafficking den that was being operated by Major Talwar and his high-level business benefactors. The names of Vasudeva Patel and Durgacharan Mahesh floated in the air but without any solid proof. Even though Vasudeva was a resident of Kolkata, Durgacharan was based out of Mumbai and was much more difficult to touch. Finally, ACP Bakshi made a breakthrough and gathered solid proof against all the accused and was all set to put an end to the heinous racket. Then, the unthinkable happened! A mole within our system informed the criminals and they used their powers to erase all evidence and killed ACP Bakshi and his team. This mole was Shahnawaz Khan! He went astray and saved his own life. However, later he returned to fool you and Ujjwal and end my ultimate mission! I think he suspected that I am behind whatever has been happening.'

'What are you saying?' exclaimed Savitri, 'Is that why he got killed? Was it a murder and not an accident?'

'Ujjwal was part of ACP Bakshi's team, but he was not aware of the deceit of Shahnawaz Khan. Ujjwal didn't know I was the secret agent. He loved me as a senior and respected me. The incident that took place at his house was not meant to harm him. I tried my best! However, he was the victim of collateral damage!'

Savitri stared at Arun with disbelief while he continued, 'When the mission was scrapped, Commissioner Mahadev Kanti was removed from office and I was left completely despondent. Commissioner Chauhan replaced him. Jai, my old friend, joined as his junior. Even though I had been his close disciple, Commissioner Chauhan knew nothing about the secret mission at Baghmundi. For the last five years, Commissioner Chauhan and Jai had been overseeing the North and North Suburban Divisions and were totally unaware about whatever had been going on inside the city. When the two of them came back, I thought I would be able to confide in them. However, the threats from the multiple killings and political pressure made me apprehensive. So, I decided to remain silent. However, the unlawful practices I engaged in, to protect my cover, started to work against me and began to erode the trust of Commissioner Chauhan and Jai.'

Savitri kept listening, recording the entire conversation in her mobile phone. Arun kept talking, 'Meanwhile, there was something else that took priority in my life. Radha was going to give birth to our first child. I was overwhelmed with joy but also knew that now I had to be more cautious about the safety of my family. I slowly distanced myself from the entire Baghmundi episode. I admit that I became selfish and maybe that is why I was punished by the Almighty!'

Arun wiped away the sweat from his forehead and continued, 'Radha got admitted to the Pink Paradise Hospital before the delivery date. The two of us had dreamt of naming our child Devi if it was a girl, or Dev if it was a boy. The child was the answer to our prayers and the divine symbol of our love. However, I was unaware that the fangs of the evil were spread everywhere! The devils from whom I was running away were following me like an elusive shadow. The Pink Paradise Hospital, too, was clandestinely owned by Durgacharan Mahesh and Vasudeva Patel and the duo was engaged in organ trafficking. It was all a part of the million-dollar smuggling business that these criminals were operating under the disguise of health services. Nobody knew that Matron Anita Gorai, who was in charge of the institute, was the one overseeing these criminal activities. I never suspected it while I was secretly investigating the Baghmundi case. So, we were unaware of the fact that even the Pink Paradise Hospital was one of their dens! Sadly, the demons of Baghmundi refused to spare us. The patient who occupied the bed adjacent to Radha was terminally ill. One night, he was brutally operated up on and robbed off his kidneys and liver. The doctors declared him dead and stated the cause to be his terminal disease! Radha was a witness to this entire episode and confided in Matron

Anita Gorai and a junior nurse Shantibala the following day. Radha was unaware that Anita Gorai was herself a partner in the crimes. However, even before she could reveal anything to me, Anita Gorai ordered for an assault on Radha.'

Arun paused a bit and then continued again, 'Dr Amitava Guha was brought in as an anaesthetist who injected a poison into Radha's body, which suddenly made her critical. Unable to fathom any specific reason for this abrupt complication, the gynaecological surgeon who was supervising Radha decided to go for an immediate operation. The five-hour-long operation couldn't save Radha's life. The poison had left no trace in her body! I have my reasons to believe that he injected her with Digitalis, which can only be accessed by doctors. This drug is used to increase contractility of the heart. But if you give it in high dose, it can cause cardiac arrhythmia that leads to a deadly ventricular tachycardia. This poison is also almost impossible to detect in blood. Unfortunately, I don't have enough evidence to prove it.

'Anita Gorai and her evil accomplices succeeded in their plans. However, Devi was born amid this whirlwind! The poison made her fragile and underdeveloped. I was shattered by this catastrophe and my whole world collapsed. After a few days, one night, a frightened Shantibala met me and revealed everything to me. I was angry and desperate and asked her to help me. But, the criminals silenced her within a few days! They had sensed that she had revealed their secrets to somebody. However, they were unable to trace me. I understood that Devi and I were in danger too! I faked the death of my child and spread the rumour that the underdeveloped baby had died within a few days after being discharged from the hospital. I became more desperate to save Devi's life, my only family in this whole world! I intentionally tarnished my name in the police department and fled. Commissioner Chauhan was disappointed in me and Jai became estranged. I didn't care, for my only aim was to save my child. I ensured that Devi remained in a hidden location, safe and away from all dangers, while I took up the blames of dishonesty and stayed away. Yet, I continued my investigation independently. Helplessly, I saw Dr Amitava Guha and Anita Gorai run away. I saw Durgacharan Mahesh exit from the country. I was helpless! I tried to write anonymous letters to newspapers like the *Kolkata Chronicle*, hoping that some investigation would take place. However, nothing worked out. I became despondent and disheartened about the administrative system and the entire functioning of our society! There was so much crime, yet the power of money enabled Durgacharan and Vasudeva to escape all punishment! My whole world was shattered and all my happiness was burnt to ashes. I lost my wife, my daughter was far away from me, my honour was tarnished and I was left astray like a mongrel. With a heart full of remorse, I decided to form my own army. I roped in people like me who had been wronged by these criminals. Soon, I had a team of five people. Some of them were family members of those who lost their lives in connection with the Baghmundi case. I trained this team and placed them as moles inside the entire administrative system and waited for the right moment to strike!'

Arun's eyes were red with anger and sorrow as he kept talking, 'When the extradition case of Durgacharan surfaced, I decided to play my cards! I knew that this was my best chance. I took it upon myself as my duty to punish these criminals. It is my duty towards Devi. My team discovered that Vasudeva Patel was trying to buy out indemnity for Durgacharan and we decided to end this drama! We sought revenge and worked hard to understand what was being planned to save Durgacharan!'

Arun looked blankly at the ceiling and said, 'My team and I worked hard and discovered that Vasudeva Patel was trying his luck with lawyers and we understood that things were going out of hand. I confronted him in the disguise of a lawyer and in a fit of anger…I killed him and wrote the word "Devi" with his blood! I thought that this would stop the endeavour to save Durgacharan but to our surprise, we found out that there were more people involved in this entire plan. The associates of Durgacharan were arranging the theft of multiple priceless artifacts to buy out indemnity for him! One such artefact, and the most valuable one, was the Bhavani Shankha! I arrived inside the bank, on the night of the theft, but found that somebody had already stolen the conch shell! That was the deed of the person disguised as a hijab-clad woman. I failed to catch that person but punished the security guards, who were also the culprits! Every revenge I took was for Devi and I left my mark, so that a warning could be sent to the entire world and Durgacharan that doomsday was near!'

Savitri interrupted, 'You killed so many people! I cannot believe it, Arun!'

Arun replied, 'I am not a killer! I am a crusader. I did everything for justice! It is justice that has been delayed for so long. It is now or never! Yes, I finished Bikash Talukdar and took Major Talwar to his doom! My team had worked meticulously to pass every information to the police department, but they were unable to decode the hidden clues!'

Savitri again interrupted, 'And who used to call you over the phone? Who was that anonymous caller?'

'It was one of my team members!' replied Arun. 'The voice was masked and expertly bypassed through the telecom networks, so that the number remained untraceable!'

'You used me too!' Savitri started to cry. 'You made me a scapegoat and utilized my innocent love and trust! I feel cheated…'

'I didn't cheat you, Savitri,' Arun came near Savitri and whispered, 'I have told you everything tonight. I never wanted to hide anything from you. I know that I will be punished for what I have done. However, I don't have any regrets. I confided in you tonight, and I am happy now! My heart feels light…'

'Why are you telling me everything?' Savitri asked in an apprehensive voice. 'Will you kill me too? I know too much now and I will be a threat to you and your team!'

'No, Savitri,' replied Arun with a dry smile, 'Somewhere, I feel your true love for me. I told you everything tonight because…when I am gone from this world, I want you to take care of Devi. I can only request you. The decision is yours... would you be Devi's mother and protect her?'

Savitri couldn't control herself anymore. She cried out loudly and hugged Arun. Tears poured down Arun's eyes, too. Savitri managed to wipe away her tears and said, 'Arun, I don't know what is in store for you. I fear, something very tragic! However, I have loved you with all my being. I promise you... I will be Devi's mother and I will protect her forever!'

'If you ever seek her,' said Arun, 'You will find Devi in the Lap of Mother Durga, inside the Tank of Turmeric!'

'What do you mean?' enquired Savitri, 'Is this another riddle?'

'The day you seek her, you will find her by remembering my words!' Arun said with a smile. 'I think you must leave now. The driver will drop you back home. Don't try to find me. I will come back at the right time!'

'Is Durgacharan in your custody? Where have you taken him? Is he still alive?' asked Savitri.

'Yes, Durgacharan is in a safe place. Don't worry, I won't kill him. He will confess his every misdeed and then go to jail. Now come, the car is waiting outside. You must hurry. It is nearly dawn,' Arun said and got up from his seat.

As the duo came out from the house, Savitri hugged Arun one last time and boarded the car. As the vehicle drove out, she stopped the voice recorder of her mobile phone and sat quietly. A tornado was brewing within her. Should she tell everything to Commissioner Chauhan or remain silent? Should she write about everything in her report? Should she try to stop Arun

Devi

from committing further crimes or should she try to help him? All these questions exhausted her. In her emotional turmoil, Savitri felt the gush of fresh wind as she uttered silently, 'I am your mother...Devi.'

While Maha Navami unfolded and a new dawn was about to break, the residents of Kolkata were already feeling the customary melancholia. The thought that Ma Durga will soon begin her journey back to Kailash and the annual mega festival would come to an end brought in a sense of sadness. Within the hearts of Savitri and Arun, a similar melancholy was brewing. Would the day bring in a mixture of happiness and sorrow as a final goodbye or was something sinister still imminent?

∞

Jai sat on a couch in front of Chauhan while the latter muttered, 'Pink Paradise!'

In the late hour of the night, the two officers were sitting in the living room in Commissioner Chauhan's house. Jai was puzzled by the Commissioner's attitude and was restless to understand what was going on in his mind. Soon, it would be the day of Maha Navami.

Commissioner Chauhan sat down on the sofa and said, 'Jai, there is something you must know! As I sat in my office this evening and pondered, a rush of old memories flashed my mind and I suddenly remembered something...Pink Paradise!'

'What is that?' asked Jai inquisitively.

'Remember Dr Amitava Guha's last words?' asked Chauhan. 'He could utter two words… Paradise and Pink! Jai, Pink Paradise is a hospital in Kolkata.'

'Sir, I am not sure what you are trying to say!' replied Jai with a perplexed expression.

'Jai, you know Arun was pretty close to me. His wife Radha was admitted for the delivery of their child in the Pink Paradise Hospital two years ago! Moreover, Dr Amitava Guha was her anaesthetist.'

Jai jumped up from his seat and exclaimed, 'What are you saying? I can't believe it!'

'Listen to this now…' Chauhan added, 'Radha, Arun's wife, once told me during a social gathering that if her first child were a girl, she and Arun would name her…Devi!'

'This is unbelievable! What are we supposed to understand?' Jai was perplexed.

'I don't know what to say! All I can understand is that Arun has a deep-rooted connection with the crimes that have been unfolding in the city,' Chauhan replied, adding 'I had somehow forgotten about this until now!' 'He continued, 'Moreover, have you observed that Arun is the only one receiving calls from the anonymous caller? Why? I strongly believe that Arun himself had devised this plan and, being a master in handling technical details, he was able to camouflage the calls!'

'So, Arun used us to get back into the police department and commenced his secret plans!' Jai had to sit down to catch his breath.

Devi

'I don't know how far we can blame Arun. However, he is definitely involved in it,' Chauhan added. 'Think carefully, during most of the crimes, Arun had been absent! Devi is the missing link! I don't know the exact motive behind his involvement in this crime and what is his link with all these people who were murdered. I don't know what his connection is with Durgacharan Mahesh, but I will find out! Remember, we need to confront him. However, I am sure he will not be an easy catch. We need to do what I had asked you to! The central government forces are spreading their web throughout and are combing the city. However, my intuition tells me that this game will not end so easily!'

'Sir, your plan will be carried out this morning! The task will be completed. I must leave now. Please rest awhile. Meanwhile, I will go home. There is a lot of thinking we need to do.'

'Yes Jai. Go home and take some rest. I will focus on our next steps. I think we are on the right track now. God knows what will happen next…'

∞

After getting back inside her apartment, Savitri made a phone call to Arun. She said, 'I have reached home. Listen, there is something that I want to tell you…'

Arun replied, 'Yes Savitri. Tell me.'

Savitri responded, 'Arun, leave everything behind and surrender to the police. Hand Durgacharan over to them and confess your crimes. At least, your life will be spared! I don't want you to die! Together we will take care of Devi. I have promised you, I will be her mother. However, I need you to be there beside me! Please Arun, please…'

Arun waited momentarily and said, 'Savitri, I know how much you love me and I know that you will protect Devi. However, I cannot end this battle. I have to finish it. It was I who opened up this can of worms and thus it is upon me to finish this ordeal. Durgacharan will get his punishment and the world will see him confess his crimes. It is only then that justice will be meted out completely. I will not surrender. I don't know what is in store for me. I don't know whether I will live or die. I only know that before it all ends, I must win this war! The justice of Ma Durga must be doled out to the demons. From this moment onwards, my phone will be unavailable and I will remain untraceable. I will get in touch with you at the right time and promise you that the ultimate revelation will happen soon!'

Savitri remarked, 'My mind tells me to reveal everything to Commissioner Chauhan as my moral duty, but my heart is saying something else. I don't know what to do. Please forgive me Arun if I have to act against you. It will be only to save your life!'

Arun finished, 'I will not stop you from doing anything. However, remember one thing, I will complete this ultimate task!'

The phone line got disconnected and Savitri sat blankly, not oblivious to the war being waged between her mind and heart.

∞

The new dawn of Maha Navami unfolded with festivities galore. It was the penultimate day of Durga Puja. While everybody prepared for the day with great excitement, the administrative departments were on their heels. The officials of the CBI and the CID were working closely with the Home Minister and the Kolkata Police in searching for Durgacharan Mahesh. The kidnapping was gaining international prominence and becoming a political issue. Newspapers were flooded with rumours and the residents of Kolkata were gulping down this overload of stories along with their first cup of morning tea. The story of Devi and her victims was making headlines and creating an environment of chaos and uncertainty.

The following day, on Maha Dashami, most of the idols of the goddess would make a beeline and everybody would head towards the ghats of the Hooghly River for the immersion of the idols. Nobody knew what was in store for Durgacharan Mahesh and his nemesis, Devi.

∞

Inside the conference room of the police headquarters, journalists had gathered for an urgent meeting. Savitri, too, had received the hurried invitation and had managed to reach the premises just in time. It was nine in the morning and the entire room was charged with anticipation. Jai arrived along with three other senior officers. Chauhan was busy in a meeting with authorities from the state government, Home Ministry, the CBI and the CID. The Spanish authorities demanded swift action and expressed their discomfort regarding the entire affair. The administrative machinery needed to function in rapid action.

A few reporters clicked photographs and some others video-recorded the meeting, while Jai took up the microphone and began his speech, 'We have been able to make significant progress in this case. Commissioner Chauhan is in a meeting with the top officials and is now discussing the next steps. We can expect rapid movement in this case. Constable Ujjwal Roy, who was injured in a blast a few days ago, and was in a state of coma, has regained his consciousness. This is great news, as he has expressed his desire to reveal something significant regarding this case. He was working covertly and had received significant intelligence but was unfortunately injured and rendered helpless. However, today, right after this meeting, Commissioner Chauhan and I will visit him at the hospital and record his statement. We expect vital information and hope that Ujjwal Roy's words will take us a step ahead in this case. On behalf of the entire police department, I promise to recover Durgacharan Mahesh from his abductors and bring the criminals behind the bars!'

The meeting was dismissed and the media people began to disperse. Savitri waited for some more time and when the crowd had significantly subsided, she walked up to Jai.

Jai looked at Savitri's anxious face and commented, 'Savitri, why are you looking so worried?'

Trying to calm down her inner turmoil, she replied, 'No, I am alright. I was just worried about whatever is happening. It is good to hear that Ujjwal Roy is recovering and I hope that he reveals something significant.'

In her mind, Savitri pondered about what Ujjwal was about to say. Had he found something in the files from the Police Quarantine Archives? Was he about to reveal everything about Arun? Her mind was in a whirlwind.

Jai understood that something seemed off with Savitri. He didn't ask anything but decided to keep an eye on her. He asked, 'Did you meet Arun today? Or did you speak with him? I have been trying to call him but his phone seems unreachable.'

'No,' exclaimed Savitri. 'I have not heard from him either. In fact, I am anxious thinking about his safety. In any case, I will not hold you back. Let me head towards my office. The online edition needs to be updated with the latest news. Do call me if you need anything.'

'Take care, Savitri', replied Jai. 'Call me if you hear from Arun. I will keep you posted about the progress on this case.'

As Savitri left, Jai asked one of his aides to follow her and keep a close watch on her. He himself headed back to the Commissioner's office. Jai had done what the Commissioner had asked him to do. Now, they would need to wait and watch how the bait worked. Chauhan was still in the meeting with the administrative officials and Jai waited patiently inside his chamber; his mind diverted to Savitri and he decided to confront her. He made up his mind that he would meet her in the evening and coax her into speaking.

∞

Inside a dingy room of the abandoned factory, Arun watched the media coverage of the press conference on one of the news channels. His jaws hardened and he murmured, 'Ujjwal Roy should not speak with the authorities. If he utters something by mistake, it will jeopardize our entire mission! Under pressure from the officials, he might reveal things that he might not under normal circumstances…'

Arun was unaware of the conversation between Chauhan and Radha, that she wished to name her child Devi. In the most desperate moments, the human mind sometimes gets rendered weak and Arun was unable to see the bait that the Commissioner had cleverly planted to catch him and his team.

An accomplice standing beside Arun commented agitatedly, 'Now, what should we do? What is your plan?'

'Sammarth,' replied Arun after a bit of hesitation, 'Ujjwal must be silenced. His death will be his sacrifice for a noble cause. Go and do the needful. Remember the face of your mother. Shantibala was a pious lady, but she was heinously trampled by these criminals. Whatever you do would not tarnish your piety. I am sure that your mother will bless you and God will forgive you!'

Sammarth looked at Arun, shook hands with him and before leaving said, 'I will not fail you in my duty! Even if I perish, I will avenge my mother's murder. Sir, I will accomplish this job successfully and Ujjwal Roy will not speak.'

Devi

Sammarth hurried out and Arun sat on a chair and closed his eyes. He needed to think about his next steps. Time was passing, soon the police would zero in on him and his team. Before that happened, Durgacharan needed to confess and Arun had to reach his ultimate goal.

∞

Chauhan returned to his chamber and spoke with Jai, 'Now that we have revealed about Ujjwal Roy, I want you to go to the hospital immediately. Make sure nobody harms him. Capture anybody who seems like a suspect. You have to be very cautious.'

After Jai left, Chauhan summoned a junior officer and asked him to bring Akhilesh Ganguly and Pranav Ganguly to the interrogation room.

The two brothers sat down and Chauhan sat opposite to them. He had a plan—he wanted to test his theory on these two men who had significant involvement in the case. Jai closed the door, locked it from within and stood in front of it. Chauhan composed his thoughts and said, 'The two of you have not fully cooperated with the police. I regret that we have to drag you further into the case, as it is getting more and more complicated! The Bhavani Shankha has still not been recovered and we have to book you for conspiracy and supporting a fugitive.'

Akhilesh replied anxiously, 'Please believe me! We have revealed everything. We don't know anything further. I swear on my family that we don't know where the conch shell is! We are not lying. Please don't drag us further, we don't want our family name to be tarnished!'

Chauhan maintained his reserved attitude and replied, 'Sorry. I cannot help you. On the day my officers first interrogated you, we received a message about your whereabouts from somebody in your family. It is clear that you've hidden some information from us. I might try to help you only if you reveal everything.'

Akhilesh covered his face and started to cry. All that could be heard in the room was the sound of his sobs. Chauhan sat quietly, waiting for something to be revealed.

Presently, Pranav broke his silence and spoke impatiently, 'Stop crying, Dada! I cannot take this torture anymore. Commissioner sir, I confess… I know who has the conch shell!'

Chauhan sat up with a jerk while Akhilesh looked wildly at his brother. Pranav continued, 'Pedro Gustav, the international smuggler, has the Bhavani Shankha! He is coordinating the sale of the artefact and the deal will be done shortly.'

'How do you know that!' exclaimed Akhilesh. He was completely shocked by this revelation. Pranav sat down near the feet of his elder brother and sobbed, 'It was I who gave that note and made the phone call to the police to make things more complicated. Dada, I became greedy, I admit. I wanted to fool you. I conspired with Major Talwar and helped pass the Bhavani Shankha to Pedro Gustav! Dada, I kept you in the dark, so that I could pocket the entire profit.'

Akhilesh was furious, 'You cheated me! I cannot believe this. You have led us to our doom!'

Pranav started crying and said, 'Please forgive me, Dada. Commissioner Chauhan, Pedro Gustav is hiding in Kolkata. He will sell the conch shell tonight. He will be there at the Ananda Mela Shopping Complex to finish the task. If you are able to capture him, then the Bhavani Shankha will be saved. This is the only piece of information that I had suppressed. Now, I have told you everything.'

Chauhan sighed, 'Very well. If you speak the truth and we are able to recover the Bhavani Shankha, I will do my best to help you.'

Pranav hugged his brother Akhilesh and the duo continued to cry again. Akhilesh was only able to say, 'Thank you, Sir…'

Chauhan came out from the interrogation room and went inside his chamber. He took out his phone, called Jai and said, 'Jai, don't say anything, just listen. Pedro Gustav, the notorious drug peddler, is about to smuggle the Bhavani Shankha tonight at the Ananda Mela Shopping Complex. We need to catch him red-handed! After you finish your work, contact me immediately and we would chalk out a plan!'

Outside the chamber of the Commissioner, inside a secluded corner of the Police Headquarter, the junior officer made a secret phone call, 'Arun sir…the notorious smuggler Pedro Gustav will be at the Ananda Mela Shopping Complex this evening to smuggle the *Bhavani Shankha*.'

Jai was at the hospital where Ujjwal was admitted. He disconnected the call after talking to the Commissioner and stood quietly at a corner of the corridor outside Ujjwal's cabin.

Maha Navami

A junior doctor arrived at the door; it was Sammarth in disguise. Jai became sceptical and quietly came and stood beside him. Sammarth understood the move and quietly entered the room. Jai winked at the constable on duty and both of them entered the room and stood by the wall. Ujjwal was lying silently on the bed, still unconscious.

This is my only chance. I need to act fast. I won't be able to escape. I cannot fear for my life; it is my duty I need to adhere to! Sammarth thought.

He closed his eyes and within a flash of a second, he took out an injection from his apron and pounced on Ujjwal like an angry lion. Jai was ready and responded swiftly. With the force of a ferocious bear, Jai pulled Sammarth away and threw the injection away from his hand with a hard punch! The constable pulled Sammarth away from the bed and pinned him down on the ground. Sammarth screamed in anger while a few more officers rushed into the cabin.

Jai took out his service revolver, held it against Sammarth's forehead and said, 'Your game is over! You are being arrested for attempted murder! Take him away.'

The heated scene created quite a ruckus inside the hospital. Three officers pulled away Sammarth and flung him inside a van.

Jai took out his mobile phone and informed Commissioner Chauhan about the arrest and everything that went down. He quickly briefed the officers on duty to guard Ujjwal. Then, he got into his jeep and rushed towards the police headquarters.

In another part of the city, Savitri sat in her cabin and

wondered, *What am I supposed to do? What is my duty now?* Her head was hurting due to the increasing tension and she was unable to focus on anything. Finally, she decided to do what was right. *I cannot betray my city. I love Arun and will always love him. However, my duty as a citizen comes first. I shall protect Devi, but I cannot let Arun commit more crimes. I must meet the Commissioner and inform him about everything.*

∞

Arun stood in front of Durgacharan and spoke, 'So, Pedro Gustav is your pawn. He is selling the precious artefacts to siphon off the money to buy you indemnity! But Devi knows everything. She knows about your activities in Baghmundi. She knows about your heinous racket in Pink Paradise! She knows about all your merciless killings! Now, it is your time to die…'

With his eyes still blindfolded, a terrorized Durgacharan replied, 'Please don't kill me! Please… I will do whatever you say. I will give you anything you ask for!'

'I don't want money! I want justice. Devi wants justice. Confess your crimes and she will perhaps spare you your life!' replied Arun. 'Tell the world about your crimes. Tell them that you are the mastermind behind all these misdeeds. You have wronged many and they are all awaiting justice!'

'I will confess! Just tell me what to do,' blurted out Durgacharan.

'Very well,' answered Arun, 'Soon you will be asked to speak in front of the entire world and you must admit your crimes. However, before that, Pedro Gustav needs to get his due! I will return to you tonight and that is when you will get your last chance to save your life.'

∞

Inside the closed quarters of the police headquarters, Chauhan, Jai and a few more officers sat around a table. Sammarth was handcuffed and made to sit on a chair opposite them. Jai came forward and slapped Sammarth hard in the face. Before Sammarth could understand anything, Jai hit him two more times and stood beside him with red eyes.

'Why did you try to kill Ujjwal Roy? Who are you working for?' Chauhan demanded to know.

Sammarth recovered from the initial shock but kept quiet. Chauhan repeated his question but the silence didn't break. Jai and another officer threw a few more blows at him. Sammarth winced in pain and panted for breath.

Chauhan asked again, 'Why do you want to kill Ujjwal Roy?'

Sammarth looked up and silently said, 'The Devi will ensure justice. You cannot make me speak. Ujjwal Roy will not be able to help you. The demons will be punished.'

Chauhan came out from the interrogation room, along with Jai and another senior officer. A junior officer came up to them and said, 'Background verification reveals that his name is Sammarth Desai. He is the son of a deceased nurse Shantibala

Desai who used to work in a hospital named Pink Paradise. This boy is currently unemployed.'

Chauhan looked at the senior officer and said, 'Take him into remand. Ask your team to interrogate him thoroughly. He might break under pressure. We must keep trying that.'

As the senior officer left, Chauhan looked at Jai and said, 'Pink Paradise! There is something associated with this place that connects Sammarth with Arun. Let us find out this hidden connection of Pink Paradise with all the key characters…Arun, Sammarth, Radha and Durgacharan Mahesh.'

Jai nodded in agreement and replied, 'I will ask my team to look for the connection. Meanwhile, I think it is time we head towards the Ananda Mela Shopping Complex.'

'Yes, Jai', responded Chauhan. 'Pedro Gustav must be intercepted. Recovering the Bhavani Shankha is of paramount importance! I have spread my secret web to rope in as much information as possible. I am sure I would have all my answers by tomorrow morning.'

Jai, Chauhan and four more officers disguised themselves in common clothes and left for the Ananda Mela Shopping Complex. The time was 5.00 p.m. and the entire place was bustling with activity. Chauhan had showed different pictures of Pedro Gustav to his officers, so that he could be easily identified and nabbed.

As time passed, the officers dispersed within the crowd, their sharp eyes scrutinizing every passing person. By the time the hour hand of the clock touched six, the crowd multiplied manifold. On the eve of Maha Navami, the revelry was beginning to peak.

Among the crowd, another man quietly stood near the staircase. He wore a maroon turban and had thick black beard. Dark coloured thick-rimmed glasses adorned his eyes. He wore a grey-coloured T-shirt and carried a little, brown bag. From this simple disguise, it was impossible to identify the man himself… but it was Pedro Gustav.

On the floor near the parapet of the first-floor balcony, a beggar in ragged clothes sat and stared at the passing crowd. He lifted his hands at everyone who went past him, in the hope of some generous alms. Nobody cared about this frail old beggar; nobody knew he was Arun Palit in disguise. His shrewd eyes saw through the indistinguishable camouflage of Pedro Gustav, but he patiently waited for something to happen.

Pedro Gustav brushed past Chauhan and said a polite 'Sorry…'

This encounter didn't raise any alarm for Chauhan. Pedro smiled and walked up to meet the person for whom he had been waiting. Arun saw the exchange and his impatience grew stronger as he wondered, *How could Commissioner Chauhan not identify Pedro?*

Pedro went and stood in front of a stranger and shook hands with him. Taking a quick look around, he slowly raised the bag to hand it over. Arun understood the signal and like a flash of lightning, took out a revolver and shot two rounds. One bullet struck Pedro on his right arm while the other brushed past the shoulder of the stranger. The two men screamed in pain and fell down on the ground due to the impact of the bullets. A sudden pandemonium gripped the entire area and the maddening crowd started running hither and thither.

Chauhan, Jai and the three officers rushed up to the victims. The turban on Pedro's head had fallen off and he was writhing in pain. Commissioner looked at his face and exclaimed, 'Pedro Gustav!'

Jai screamed at his officers, 'Quick… Arun must be around! The shot was so accurate that I strongly feel that it can only be fired by a man of his expertise! Two of you comb the area to find him while one of you call for backup and ambulance!'

Chauhan picked up the bag and took out its content. Jai stood beside him and the two stared at it with wide open eyes for what was inside was the real Bhavani Shankha!

'Please don't kill me! Sir, please don't kill me… I will give you everything I have!' howled Pedro as blood oozed from his wound as he lay on the ground.

Jai looked at the other man and said, 'I know this person! He is Sushant Kesav, the moderator at Cigna Art Gallery! I have seen him on multiple occasions during art exhibitions.'

Police backup arrived soon and Pedro and Sushant were carried away to the ambulances. Arun had made a swift escape. The two officers searched for him in vain and returned empty handed. The backup forces worked hard and controlled the chaos within the premises of the Ananda Mela Shopping Complex. The scare amongst the revellers got diluted but the news spread like wildfire all around the city.

Chauhan and Jai returned to the police headquarters with

plans to interrogate Pedro Gustav and Sushant Kesav the next day and extract any vital knowledge they could.

As Jai was about to leave, Chauhan interrupted him and said, 'Jai…did you see the old beggar near the parapet of the first-floor balcony of Ananda Mela Shopping Complex?'

Jai expressed a perplexed look and said, 'What do you mean, Sir? Who was it?'

'It was Arun in disguise!' answered Chauhan calmly. 'And he shot the bullets!'

Jai was even more agitated and asked, 'Then why did you let him go? What is going on?'

Chauhan replied, 'Jai, I have groomed him during his training. I know him more than anybody else. Remember, this Devi case is not just a sequence of crimes…it is a perception, it is an ailment that needs to be cured. I didn't let Arun escape. I am trying to eradicate the disease! Trust me, everything will be solved tomorrow! Tonight, I will try to uncover what is still in the dark. Tomorrow, the final revelation will happen. Be patient till then and have faith in me, my boy… I will ask you to question Arun at the right time!'

Jai replied, 'I trust you, Sir. I will do everything in my power to not let you down.'

Chauhan ended the conversation with, 'After interrogating Sammarth tonight, free him and let him go…'

Jai looked at Chauhan's face and understood that he should not question further. He smiled and left saying, 'Yes Sir.'

∞

At 11.00 p.m., Arun came and stood beside Durgacharan Mahesh and said, 'Tomorrow, on Maha Dashami, you have a big task ahead of you. Tomorrow, you have to confess about Baghmundi, about Pink Paradise and every other crime you have committed. Only then Devi will spare you before she departs from this city! Be prepared. Think what you will say. You will have fifteen minutes. One more hour and it will be Maha Dashami... Tomorrow morning, your confession and revelation of the truth will finally bring the justice sought by Devi...'

Maha Dashami

Inside the premises of the abandoned factory, Arun sat down with four other men. He looked at their faces and said, 'We had started a war together against the wrongdoings of Durgacharan Mahesh. However, I was the torchbearer and you all were always by my side. Now the time has come to dissolve this team. So far, we managed to remain obscure and invisible, but now is the time when you all should return to your normal lives. I will take the last step…the final stride to finish this journey, but I cannot sacrifice your lives for it. Sammarth was arrested but was released. This was a signal for me by the Commissioner. He knows I am behind this! If I still continue to keep you all involved, then the CBI will definitely find you. I cannot let that happen!'

One of the men interrupted, 'Arun, we cannot let you face the music alone! We had all vowed to avenge the deaths of our loved ones. Why will you face the dangers alone?'

'It was I who recruited you,' shouted Arun, 'and I am

dismissing you! Listen to me, don't be stubborn. If anything happens to me, you will be alive to continue the crusade against evil. Please, please understand my plea! I promise you that Durgacharan will be brought to justice!' Arun looked at the faces of the four men, got up from his seat and continued, 'Before dawn, leave this city and go away! Go to a faraway place, settle down and lead a happy life. Promise me…please promise me!'

The four men, charged with emotions, stood up and said together, 'We promise you, Arun! Your sacrifice will be remembered!'

∞

Chauhan picked up his phone and dialled a number. He said, 'Savitri, this is Commissioner Chauhan speaking. Can you please hurry down to my office? It is urgent!'

Savitri replied, 'Yes Sir. I am coming right away.'

Next, Chauhan made a phone call to Jai, 'Come to my office right now. There is something that we must discuss.'

Jai responded with an alert, 'Right Sir. I am coming immediately.'

It was five in the morning, the morning of Maha Dashami. It was the final day of the Durga Puja festivities when every resident of Kolkata gets soaked in the mixed emotions of nostalgia, melancholy and jubilation. It was an emotional day for all devotees, as they were set to bid farewell to their beloved Ma Durga. Her idols were to to be taken towards the ghats of Hooghly for immersion. Everything had been decided even before the break of dawn. The Traffic Police were prepared for the revelry. The government and administrative leaders were vigilant about the rescue of Durgacharan Mahesh. The central government forces and the CBI team were scattered all across the city. The stories of Devi and the fugitive business baron loomed like a shadow over every person in the city.

Within the next thirty minutes, Savitri and Jai were sitting inside Chauhan's chamber. The first rays of the morning sun were slowly spreading across the horizon, but inside the closed quarter of Chauhan's chamber, an intricate web of truth was about to unfold.

Chauhan began, 'Today, at the brink of a new dawn, I will reveal the truth!' Savitri and Jai looked at Chauhan with eagerness as the latter continued, 'The case of Devi is an intriguing one and has multiple facets that make it even more difficult to fathom. It all began on Mahalaya with the murder of the high-profile businessman Vasudeva Patel before his brother-in-law Durgacharan Mahesh was about to be extradited from Spain to India. In the middle of Durga Puja festivities, it led to an unrest. However, things didn't stop at this. Next, the Bhavani Shankha was stolen and three security guards were murdered on Maha Chaturthi. The following day, on Maha Panchami, Durga Puja inaugurations began with grandeur but the chief minister's secretary, Mr Talukdar, was brutally murdered inside a plush hotel room. Arun theorized that each crime scene clue was somehow associated with one of the weapons of Goddess

Durga...conch shell, sword, bow and arrow, and so on. Another weird thread that connected everything was the word "Devi"!'

Chauhan took a quick look around and continued, 'That night, Durgacharan Mahesh arrived in the city under the canopy of tight security. He was moved to a high-security bungalow in Alipore. On Maha Shashti, Major Talwar was poisoned and murdered inside the stadium, and Samuel Gomes was mysteriously murdered near Paria House during the police operation being led by Jai and Arun. Late in the night, an anonymous elusive assailant attacked Durgacharan, injured him and warned him about the wrath of Devi. We moved Durgacharan to another safe location with tighter security! On the morning of Maha Shaptami, Anita Gorai was murdered inside her apartment with a sword and Dr Amitava Guha was killed in Hotel Aston Residency. Late in the night, there was a blast in which Shahnawaz was burnt to death while Ujjwal was critically injured. Finally, on Maha Ashthami, Durgacharan was abducted and still remains untraceable!'

Jai interrupted, 'Amid all this mayhem, we find that the Bhavani Shankha we recovered was a fake. We got a tip-off from the Ganguly brothers that Pedro Gustav was smuggling the original conch shell and we were able to catch him. However, an anonymous attacker shot at him! Sir, we know all this... what is it that you are trying to say?'

Chauhan commented, 'Jai, you are correct! Remember, amid all this drama we keep getting anonymous messages that Devi seeks justice and will do anything to get it!'

Jai replied, 'Sir, what about Baghmundi and the case of ACP Bakshi? What is it that we are trying to solve?'

'If we look at the crimes separately, they seem completely unrelated. However, if we piece them together, we can find a connection. Every crime is associated with the arrival of fugitive business baron Durgacharan Mahesh! So, Devi was trying to punish all these men and pass a message that Durgacharan must not be spared! However, his trial yielded lukewarm results and before he was able to leave Kolkata, he was abducted! So, we can deduce that Devi is trying to bring justice to Durgacharan and his associates in Kolkata itself. There is something very sinister that connects all these victims to Kolkata and Durgacharan Mahesh!' Chauhan said.

Jai questioned, 'What were you saying about Arun? Sir, you left me in the dark last night…'

Chauhan sat down on his chair and spoke, 'We were fools, Jai. We couldn't see what was right in front of our eyes! During the years when you and I were posted away in the suburbs, Arun was a part of the Kolkata Police and was working with Commissioner Mahadev Kanti and ACP Bakshi. During those years, something very sinister happened and Arun and his family unfortunately became victims of it!'

Savitri's eyes lit up with fear while Jai sat speechless. Chauhan continued, 'I was in the dark until the day Dr Amitava mentioned Pink Paradise! There was something lurking in my subconscious mind that I couldn't place a finger on. I started my quest, secretly…because I didn't know whom to trust. I could feel that there was a mole inside our department who was siphoning off vital intelligence but I didn't have any proof! During this quest, I delved deeper into the dark web and found something pertinent. And, one day, I remembered the missing link too! Arun's wife Radha was admitted at the Pink Paradise Hospital before she died there! This realization crashed upon my cognizance and I started to weave the pieces together. My next goal was to understand the secret of Baghmundi.'

Jai was still speechless while tears started to roll down Savitri's eyes. Chauhan continued with the explanation, 'Amid the chaos, I could uncover one vital thing: Bhavani Shankha was being smuggled along with other priceless artefacts to buy out indemnity for Durgacharan Mahesh and Devi was trying to prevent it, so that Durgacharan could not escape the clutches of justice and was punished in Kolkata itself for his misdeeds! The question remained: who was doing all this? Remember Jai, how Arun was always absent each time the crimes were committed and how it was always him who was contacted by the anonymous caller? Remember how the messages got delivered inside my chamber or how the emails reached me? Remember how the secret location of the CBI vehicle got leaked and Durgacharan was abducted? The one man who is capable of such feat…the one and only person who has the intelligence to execute this master plan…is Arun Palit!'

'Devi is,' added Chauhan sorrowfully, 'the deceased child of Arun and Radha! It was the name they had lovingly thought of… Alas, the child died soon after Radha's demise! I carried out my secret interrogations with retired Commissioner Mahadev Kanti and a few other officers of the department who chose to remain anonymous. The revelation was startling and it helped me unearth explosive insider information. That clears the motive. Yes, I don't have any doubt about it now.'

'Now the motive…' Chauhan continued, 'Arun was a secret recruit of ACP Bakshi, who was unearthing the Baghmundi case. However, when things went awry and the stakeholders were eliminated by the criminals, Arun went undercover! Baghmundi was a human organ trafficking den operated by Major Talwar! It was like a covert headquarter that connected several notorious hospitals, doctors and peddlers of organ smuggling. It was the secret business of Vasudeva Patel and Durgacharan Mahesh! After getting out from the hideous web, Arun found a breath of fresh air when Radha was about to give birth to their first child and got admitted to the Pink Paradise Hospital. However, misfortune followed them. Alas, he was unaware that this hospital too was one of the hubs of their heinous organ theft and Radha had witnessed everything!'

Commissioner Chauhan got up from his seat in excitement and added, 'Durgacharan Mahesh and Vasudeva Patel were the secret masterminds of this crime and were sleeping partners in the Pink Paradise Hospital, and their names remained undisclosed! Matron Anita Gorai was the torchbearer and Radha had accidentally confided in her! The heartless Anita Gorai and Dr Amitava Guha conspired and led Radha to her death! It was a cold-blooded murder, camouflaged as a medical complication!

I assume that Arun got to know everything later from a junior nurse named Shantibala, who too was murdered! Sammarth is Shantibala's son!'

Chauhan continued, 'Arun was helpless and despondant and couldn't confide in anybody. He remained a speechless witness to everything! Finally, when Durgacharan's extradition was announced, Arun became active and planned the entire series of crimes! The murders of Vasudeva, the security guards, Samuel Gomes, Major Talwar and Talukdar were to either prohibit the smuggling of the conch shell or to avenge the crimes committed by them! His message was successfully delivered across the city! The revenge of Devi had spread like wildfire!'

Chauhan paused a while and mentioned, 'Arun has Durgacharan in his custody! However, I don't know how he would prove the crimes committed by that devil. I have no idea about what is he planning right now and how he wishes to mete out justice! I don't know how he will end this wildfire! All I know is one thing: we cannot stop this by simply arresting Arun. We have to stop this epidemic! The case of Devi has so many links, so many crimes associated with it! Arun had formed his army using the families of the victims of Durgacharan's atrocities, and Sammarth was one amonst them. His team is fearless and strong and they remain elusive. They must not be punished. So many people had been wronged and murdered! If we have to close this case, we have to find an elixir to heal the wounds of Devi...'

'But how do we do that Sir?' Jai was now starting to get worried.

'I believe Arun will do something to give us a signal! I just don't know how he will prove everything for which he is risking so much! We must wait for the right moment,' Chauhan replied. 'ACP Balwant Khanna from the CBI and his special team reached Kolkata last night. They have orders to storm through every lane and every street of this city to find Durgacharan. Khanna is a fierce officer and he will not stop at anything. I sincerely hope that Arun surrenders before us, before Khanna finds him. The Devi case needs to be closed at the earliest.'

Mustering some courage, Savitri finally broke her silence, 'Sir, I will not hide anything. I feel it is my moral duty to reveal the truth to you. Arun met me last night and took me to a hideout. Even though Durgacharan was not present there, I got a chance to listen to Arun's confession. Arun is unaware that I recorded the entire conversation in my phone. I hope this will act as evidence to prove his guilt. I just pray that he stays alive…'

Savitri was unable to control her tears. She took her mobile phone and switched on the recorded audio. Chauhan and Jai sat speechless and listened to Arun's tragic story. The long audio kept playing while the three people could not help but empathize with Arun despite all the crimes he had committed.

As the audio playback ended, Chauhan exclaimed, 'Devi is alive? I can't believe it! Arun's daughter is not dead? This is the best news that I have heard so far!'

Savitri smiled dryly and said, 'Yes Sir. She is alive, but Arun has kept her at a secret place. I have sworn to protect her and I shall do so till my last breath.'

Jai was equally shook on learning about Devi, 'Oh God! Devi is alive! We must protect her.'

'Jai, if we have to protect her, we must keep her existence a secret! Savitri, this audio clipping must not reach anybody. Remove it from your phone, so that it is lost forever! It is the only way in which we can protect Devi. Sooner or later, the truth about Arun and his crusade will get revealed. Durgacharan has a far-reaching villainous network. We mustn't reveal anything about Devi. Even if they get to know about Arun, they mustn't know about his daughter. Or else, to take revenge upon him, these devils might try to harm that innocent child…' Chauhan replied.

Savitri nodded her head and then deleted the recording. Jai heaved a sigh of relief while Chauhan sat down with a worried face. It was almost eight in the morning and he knew that ACP Khanna and his team had already begun their search.

Radio Jockey Mihir Dubey hurried inside the studio of Radio Masala, the most heard FM channel in Kolkata. His programme 'Morning Bites with Mihir' was about to begin sharp at nine. Mihir had been hosting the programme for over a decade and almost every resident of Kolkata tuned in to the popular radio frequency to listen to him. Throughout the days of Durga Puja festivities, Mihir had organized special talk shows with the public and had taken their opinion about how things were going on in the city. There had been talks about the revelry, the traffic

Maha Dashami

situation, the rush at pandals and about the recent drama around Devi and the ongoing crimes. Maha Dashami meant the last day of the celebration and Mihir was excited to finish his programme on Durga Puja with some flair. It was a show where listeners called with song requests or confessions or even just tidbits from their lives; everything happened in an unscripted manner and callers got a chance to speak to the RJ directly.

'Good morning, Kolkata!' Mihir delivered with an energy packed voice. 'Today, on the auspicious morning of Maha Dashami, let us listen to the first song to rejuvenate your energy! Then we will speak with our first caller and talk about the mega carnival that we have witnessed this year in our beloved city! The climate outside is overcast but I am sure that some good music will lift up everybody's mood this morning.'

Mihir played a popular retro song while thousands of listeners tuned in to his channel eagerly. After the song, he switched on the telephone line and spoke on the microphone, 'We have our first caller for the day. Let's see who is on the line…'

The telephone rang a couple of times and Mihir received it with enthusiastically, 'Hello there…who are we speaking to today?'

A male voice spoke in a sober tone, 'Good morning, Mihir. I am not a regular caller. However, this call is special, as thousands of citizens are listening to our conversation. I am the torchbearer of Devi and I have somebody very special with me now. He wants to confess something live. I request you to broadcast this, so that everyone can hear the truth!'

RJ Mihir was surprised by the call, trying to decide what should be done, while the technicians broadcasting the show were perplexed about what was about to unfold. Mihir winked at his production manager not to disconnect the call and he continued to speak, 'Alright sir... We shall listen to you. May I know who is on the line?'

'My name is immaterial... Our time is short. I implore you to keep this call connected until the confession is over. I am handing over the phone to the most coveted person in Kolkata today... the fugitive business baron, Durgacharan Mahesh!' Arun said in a single breath and handed over the phone to Durgacharan.

Arun pointed a revolver at Durgacharan and nudged him to speak, 'Time is of essence. Confess to your crimes and bring on the justice that has been delayed...'

A junior officer ran inside Chauhan's chamber and exclaimed, 'Sir, quickly turn on the radio! Durgacharan is LIVE on Radio Masala channel...' Jai and Savitri jumped up while Chauhan switched on the radio in his phone.

Mihir and the rest of the city listened spellbound while Durgacharan talked, 'My name is Durgacharan Mahesh and I am at the mercy of Devi for everything I have done! I will now confess everything before the entire city and all the listeners and beg for mercy!

Mihir asked with anxiety, 'Mr Durgacharan, where are you? Where have your abductors taken you? Please tell us...'

Durgacharan answered, 'I don't know where I am. I am not hurt, I am alright. I just want to return home! Yet, all this is immaterial now... My crimes cannot be forgiven, but I will pray to Devi and her torchbearers to spare my life. I will gladly accept any punishment that is meted out to me by law!'

The city of Kolkata came to a standstill while almost every person tuned in to the 'Morning Bites with Mihir'.

News about this high-octane drama had reached ACP Khanna and he commanded his team, 'Quick...find out the location of the caller! We are heading out right away. We must capture the criminals immediately! This is our best and only chance...'

Chauhan looked at Jai and Savitri, and said in a scared voice, 'Let's go! Jai, ask your team to get in touch with the radio station, find out the details of the call and share the location from where the call is coming. ACP Khanna must be tracing the call and will hunt down Arun! We must reach there before he and his team does!'

Keeping the radio switched on in his phone, Chauhan, along with Jai and Savitri, stormed out and got inside his car and sped away from the police headquarters. Khanna and his team of armed officers were already on the road. Within a few minutes, the location of the abandoned factory reached Chauhan as well as Khanna, and both parties rushed towards it.

Khanna spoke with his boss on call, 'Sir, with your permission, I will engage in combat with the abductors.'

The voice from the opposite end replied, 'Kill the kidnappers if you have to but rescue Durgacharan. This is an issue of national security! We cannot compromise anything. The world needs to know that we don't spare any criminal act.'

On the other hand, Chauhan spoke with Jai and Savitri, 'I know ACP Khanna will not stop. I hope we are able to do something before…'

Meanwhile, Durgacharan continued his speech: '…Throughout my life, I have engaged in many heinous acts and businesses. My fortune comprises huge wealth that I managed to garner through many such criminal activities. Using influence and money, I had always been able to escape the clutches of law! However, I could not escape the justice of Devi…' He took a deep breath and went on, 'My brother-in-law Vasudeva Patel and I chose Kolkata as one of the hubs for executing our sinister plans. I lived in Mumbai and was operating my covert businesses in Kolkata, so that my crimes remained untraceable. Initially, we began with illegal real estate businesses, but slowly our thirst for money increased and within a short time, we jumped into the lucrative industry of human organ theft and trafficking! The secret den for this was code-named Baghmundi! My trusted aide in this trade was Major Talwar, who worked as an agent and an intermediary for executing the business! I made a lot of money in this but soon ACP Bakshi followed our trail. We tried to divert him, but things went out of control. I was forced to order the extreme step… We executed ACP Bakshi and eliminated many from his team. The case was perhaps the biggest cover-up in the history of the Kolkata Police. We became dormant and shifted our operations elsewhere.'

Durgacharan paused a bit and then continued, 'However,

Maha Dashami

Baghmundi was not my only business. This lucrative trade of human organ theft and trafficking was one of the numerous businesses, thanks to which we prospered and grew. Nonetheless, the organ theft business, centrally operated from Baghmundi, fetched us a lot of money, as we were able to rope in several hospitals and their patrons. Amid them, a prime hub for our operation was the Pink Paradise Hospital. Even though this place was not a very popular one, it fetched sufficient patients we could secretly operate on, steal their organs and declare them dead due to some terminal disease. Matron Anita Gorai and a few other doctors were my aides. Every bit of the money got siphoned off through multiple bank accounts and reached me anonymously! I had bought the silence of the bank officials and nobody was suspicious of anything. I made millions and became stronger day by day. Gradually, I engaged in the smuggling of priceless artefacts and started to earn in foreign currencies. In other parts of the country, I engaged in the business of fake currency notes and again siphoned off huge sums into my bank accounts! Finally, I went ahead for the big one! I purchased the loyalties of some big officials at the nationalized banks, faked letters of credit and received huge loans in the name of business development. All that money got moved to my covert accounts and I fled from the country!'

Khanna listened to the confession over radio. His eyes didn't blink as he sat down like a stone. He was an honest officer who was committed to his duty. Nobody could gauge what was going on in his mind or heart.

In a heavy baritone, Durgacharan shouted, 'Yes, I stole money, I killed innocent people, I duped thousands of people and I cheated my nation! I know my crimes cannot be forgiven, but I plead to Devi...spare me my life! I will face every trial and accept every punishment! Please let me go home.'

Arun asked, 'How do we get the proof of your claims? How can your confessions be verified? Tell us!'

Chauhan spoke while listening, 'This is the biggest question... Let's see what Durgacharan has to say!'

Durgacharan replied in a shaky voice, 'The golden ring on my middle-finger on my right hand...that is the proof! It is not just a ring that I am wearing. Under it is engraved a hidden nano chip! I never part with this ring and this chip is usually undetected by scanning devices. All details, all proof, all evidence related to my business dealings, including the details of my bank accounts and classified police files, are stored in this chip. Please take it from me and you will be able to extract everything against me! Please spare my life... don't kill me. I plead guilty and beg for mercy from the entire city of Kolkata!'

Khanna with his team arrived near the narrow and congested lane leading to the abandoned factory where Durgacharan was being held captive. The valiant officer and six of his best men opened the safety latches of their weapons and readied themselves for action.

Arun grabbed the phone and spoke, 'I don't have much time. My name is Arun Palit and I am a police officer! I know

Maha Dashami

I have betrayed my department by taking law into my own hands. However, there is a reason behind it and everybody needs to know about it. Devi is not just one person. Devi is a perception! Devi is a revolution. Devi was my child who was a victim of human evil!'

Seized by frenzy, Arun continued talking, 'Devi is the revenge of every kin of those who were brutally murdered by Durgacharan Mahesh! Devi is the name of each person whose hard-earned money he stole! Devi is the justice that has been delayed, to cleanse this earth, this city and this country from criminals like Durgacharan Mahesh...'

He added, 'I confess that I was a secret agent recruited by ACP Bakshi to uncover the Baghmundi case, and I, helplessly, witnessed the slaughter of innocents!'

Savitri's eyes could not hold back her tears as she heard Arun's voice on the radio channel. The entire city listened to his words. 'My little world comprised my beloved Radha and our miracle child, Devi. I was helpless when they murdered Radha in the Pink Paradise Hospital to keep their heinous organ theft business alive! Throughout the years, I have suffered, without any help and watched Durgacharan escape from this country! I didn't have any proof! However, when his extradition was announced, I was determined to unite the brethren and bring to life the revenge of Devi! Yes, we have killed criminals like Vasudeva Patel, Major Talwar, Bikash Talukdar and Anita Gorai...but they were all heinous murderers and I don't regret killing them!'

Khanna and his team practically jumped out from their

vehicle and rushed inside the factory, heading towards the dingy room where Durgacharan and Arun were present. Khanna and his team knew what their orders were.

Chauhan's car pulled up inside the factory premises and the trio jumped out from the vehicle and rushed inside. Savitri was trembling with terror. Jai was bewildered by everything that had unfolded. Chauhan shouted, 'Let us be quick. ACP Khanna and his men are inside. We must hurry!'

Arun said over the call, 'This golden ring is the proof that will bring Durgacharan to justice! Maha Dashami is indeed the zenith of this long-stretched drama!' Arun pulled out the golden ring from Durgacharan's finger and looked below it. There was indeed a mini chamber that held an almost invisible golden-coloured nano chip! He held it tightly in his left fist and looked at Durgacharan.

Like a flash of lightning, Khanna and his team stormed inside the room with their weapons raised. He screamed, 'Freeze! Don't move!'

Durgacharan shouted, 'Save me, please…'

Arun momentarily looked at the men. His gun was pointed towards Durgacharan. Without delaying a second, Arun pulled the trigger! The bullet struck Durgacharan on his neck and ripped off a portion of his flesh. He uttered a faint cry, fell from his chair on to the ground.

Khanna pulled the trigger of his gun twice. Two bullets struck Arun on his chest. The impact of the gunshot was such that Arun lost hold of the gun in his hand. He moved back a few steps and stumbled upon some broken furniture. Outside, rainclouds had spread all over the sky. It was an unexpected cyclonic formation that seemed to have brewed up through divine intervention. Bolts of thunder roared with flashes of lightning. It was perhaps the wrath of Devi—a sign of the gory climax. And then, there was downpour.

'Wait, don't shoot!' Chauhan screamed just when all three of them reached where the scene was unfolding, but it was too late…

Savitri stood with her back against a wall to steady herself as she watched Arun bleed from his chest! The two wounds on Arun's body were fatal and blood gushed out through the punctures. Jai rushed to Durgacharan, who was lying in a pool of his blood. The entire city of Kolkata heard this gory affair live over radio and everything came to a standstill.

Arun's grip on his left fist slowly eased and the golden ring fell on the ground. Chauhan ran up to him along with Jai and helped him up. Savitri could barely walk up to him; her whole body was trembling like a leaf. Arun opened his eyes momentarily, looked at her and uttered, 'Devi …'

Chauhan stared at Khanna, whose team had rushed to pick up Durgacharan Mahesh. The Commissioner anxiously asked, 'Why?'

Khanna replied with a sigh that had a tinge of sadness, 'Today, we all did our duty!'

∞

Police ambulances were quick to arrive; Durgacharan and Arun were taken away. Everybody around was melancholic despite the operation being successful—the person behind the murders had been caught and Durgacharan had been found alive. Chauhan, Jai and Savitri rushed in their car to tail the ambulance taking Arun. The news had spread everywhere and the Spanish authorities too had been informed about the mission.

Arun was declared dead on arrival. He had succumbed to his injuries before he could even reach the hospital. Durgacharan was profusely bleeding and was unconscious. The doctors rushed him towards the critical care unit. Savitri sat down on a bench with a thud as Arun's lifeless body was taken away inside the mortuary. She was unable to control her emotions any longer and began to weep. Chauhan and Jai stood silently. Everyone was speechless. For the first time, tears rolled down Jai's eyes. He had just lost a friend whom he held in high regard and who was very dear to him. Media persons flocked the premises of the hospital. High ranking officials from the police department as well as the government rushed in.

After a three-hour-long surgery, the seniormost doctor came out from the operation theatre and declared, 'Durgacharan's life is out of danger now. However, I am afraid his body has been paralysed forever! The injury from the bullet had ripped off a major portion of his nerves that connects to the brain. This damage is permanent. He is unconscious as of now. We will get to know about the extent of his injuries only after he regains consciousness. Yet, there is one hope amid this…

I believe his speech and auditory organs will not be affected much and he will be able to speak and hear, but his body will remain motionless! We are shifting him to the Super Specialty Hospital for further critical care.'

Chauhan and Jai got up and the former said, 'Savitri, we are returning to the headquarters. I need to get this computer chip analysed, so that we can extract the data. The mortuary will keep Arun's body for autopsy. Please come with us. The day has been awful for all of us. You need to recover from the shock. I will drop you home on our way.'

Savitri nodded lightly, wiped away her tears and followed Chauhan and Jai.

The Home Ministry issued a statement about their successful execution of the operation as the spokesperson mentioned, 'Durgacharan Mahesh has been critically injured. He is being treated at the hospital. However, we know from our sources that he will survive! The abductor, Arun Palit, one of our officers, had engaged in combat but was wounded. He succumbed to his injuries on reaching the hospital! The explosive confessions made by Durgacharan and Arun will be investigated and the evidence that Durgacharan had handed over will be scrutinized. This is one of the biggest criminal cases in the recent past and will be definitely dealt with seriousness!'

Savitri got inside her apartment and locked the door. She sat down on the sofa and listened to the recording from her phone. She lifted her finger to delete the clipping, but something in her heart stopped her. It was the last recorded voice of Arun,

Devi

her love! She dropped the idea and kept the phone aside.

Five hours later, Chauhan and Jai received permission from the higher authorities and the Home Ministry to analyse the data on the nano chip. The two of them, along with other senior officers, reached the IT laboratory and handed over the chip to the supervising officer, Mr Shaswat. The latter placed it inside a reader. Everybody leaned forward towards the screen of the mainframe computer eagerly. Within moments, loads of data appeared and flashed across the screen.

'This is huge!' exclaimed Mr Shaswat. 'The volume of information and classified data in this chip is enough to prove everything! The details of bank accounts and other evidence will allow us to solve not only the money laundering case but also other criminal activities of Durgacharan!'

Inspector General Anant Sridharan commented, 'Shaswat, save this data securely. We have just uncovered a heap of gold! This chip will be handed over to the CBI for further investigation.'

∞

Outside, in the streets, the idol immersion carnival had begun. It was almost 6.00 p.m., and the final stage of the Durga Puja festivities was underway. The crimson hue of the setting sun flooded the corners of the huge police headquarters with a red tint that almost looked like blood.

Savitri sat on a chair in her veranda and watched the

procession of people heading towards the ghats for the idol immersion. The wind felt chilly and Savitri felt slightly feverish. She was still unable to grasp what had happened. She could not believe that Arun was no more. She got up from her chair and went inside. She sat on the sofa and switched on the television. The news media was abuzz with debates about the case. Speculations about the identity of Devi were rampant and different theories floated in the air. A CBI spokesperson, along with officials from the Home Ministry, briefed the news media about the development on the case.

In a press conference, the Home Minister said, 'Durgacharan Mahesh is a criminal. Apart from the money laundering case, his dramatic confession this morning was verified and a lot of explosive proofs are in the hands of the authorities. The government assures that justice will be meted out to the victims and their families, and the guilty will be punished!'

Jai returned home, feeling a strange emotional turbulence within. As the idol of Ma Durga was being taken away for the immersion ceremony, he looked at her distant face and uttered silently, 'Maa, your justice is so strange! To punish a demon, a good man lost everything and is now lying dead. We are helpless mortals whose hands are tied. Please bless the innocent Devi… she is your pure incarnation!'

Epilogue

The Durgacharan case dug up many hidden secrets. In the next fifteen days, seven politicians, twelve business tycoons, several underworld dons, goons and smugglers were arrested. The news media bombarded the masses with an abundance of conspiracy theories. The Ganguly brothers received their punishment for being involved in smuggling and concealing facts, along with an equal share of social embarrassment. The CBI succeeded in recovering several priceless artefacts that were being smuggled; huge money laundering sums were channelled back to the country. Pedro was finally facing trials for all his illegal activities about which police had gathered sufficient evidence. A lot was uncovered and undone, and a lot remained to be investigated and brought to justice.

Durgacharan didn't recover from the fatal blow and his body practically became a vegetable. The Spanish authorities released a press statement with words of appreciation about how the Indian authorities had handled the critical situation and how

Epilogue

justice had been meted out. Finally, the face of the nation had been saved from embarrassment in front of the entire world.

Another week later, Chauhan, Jai and Savitri attended a quiet funeral for the valiant Arun Palit. The cremation was without any fanfare. The rituals were completed a night after the doctors were through with Arun's autopsy.

After finally laying Arun to rest, the trio came out with a heavy heart and stood outside the funeral ground. Chauhan said in a grim voice, 'The government authorities didn't want to create any hype about Arun. There is a lot of involvement from the bureaucracy. After the high-profile arrests and mud pelting, the government and political fraternity have been left red-faced! However, in our country, this will also be forgotten soon. Yet the authorities want Arun's story to be under wraps. They want him to pass down history unnoticed! We are helpless. We cannot do anything. His methods might have been wrong but Arun did bring justice and that was what was necessary! The paralysed Durgacharan is locked in his own body forever! It is his prison! He will have to suffer. He will suffer every moment of his remaining life! It is perhaps the best punishment for this devil.'

Jai added with a sigh, 'I am happy that Devi's identity remained a secret! Even though Durgacharan is paralysed, his hounds will be around to hunt down any surviving family member of Arun. The world knows that she is dead. To keep the child safe, we must guard the secret that she is alive.'

Savitri added at last, 'I have lost Arun! I request you to

forget this case. I hope wherever Devi is…she is protected and is happy…'

The trio left, but an unanswered question loomed in the air.

Three months passed. Savitri sat on the stool in her balcony and stared at the passing traffic. The case of Durgacharan Mahesh had left a bitter impact on her. She had volunteered as a witness to the case. However, her bosses and the new media fraternity had not taken this with a positive spirit. The previous week, Savitri resigned from the *Kolkata Chronicle*. She didn't want to live with whispers and ridicule in the place where she worked. She knew that she had fulfilled her duty towards the man whom she had loved unconditionally. Now, she could start working on a fresh start.

The curtains of her balcony fluttered in the cool breeze of the winter morning. Arun's words reverberated in her mind…'If you ever seek her,' Arun had said, 'you will find Devi in the Lap of Mother Durga, inside the Tank of Turmeric!'

For the past three months, she had let it all mellow down. The story and buzz around Devi had subsided significantly. Such is the law of nature that even the most devastating things slowly fade away with the passage of time. Time is the best healer.

Savitri was yet to decide what she wanted to do ahead in her life. *Whatever I do, I will leave this city. Arun's memories will not let me move on if I continue living in Kolkata.*

How will I find Devi? How will I keep my last promise to Arun? What did he mean by…'in the Lap of Mother Durga'? she thought.

Epilogue

The pages of the newspaper lying on her side-table flapped in the breeze. Lost in thought, she stared at the fluttering pages. A few lines printed on a page caught her eyes and she mindlessly read those aloud, still caught in a trance.

Suddenly, one of the words seemed to stand out and she jumped from her seat exclaiming, 'Durgapur!' The name is Durgapur...that is what Arun's riddle meant by..."in the Lap of Mother Durga"!'

Savitri clasped her hands and wondered, *Devi must be somewhere in Durgapur! However, I don't know where would I be find her in Durgapur. The next piece to the riddle is perhaps in the phrase, 'inside the Tank of Turmeric'.*

Savitri went inside her apartment and paced around impatiently in the living room. Her mind was whirling, trying to decipher the riddle's final part. She translated the words to figure out the solution, 'Turmeric in Hindi is called *haldi*, while tank is called *kund*—Haldi Kund!' Savitri exhaled a sigh of relief as joy filled her soul, 'If my intuition is correct, I will have to seek a place called Haldi Kund in Durgapur!'

She looked at her watch. It was not even nine in the morning. She quickly freshened up, got dressed, packed her travel bag and left her apartment. A familiar taxi driver was standing across the road. She hired the taxi and asked the driver to rush to the railway station. She reached her destination in forty minutes, purchased a ticket and then boarded the express train that was supposed to depart from the platform at 11.40 a.m. and reach Durgapur around 3.00 p.m.

Devi

Throughout her journey, she could not think about anything else but Devi. She wondered *Will I be able to find Haldi Kund? Are my assumptions correct? How will I recognize her? She has never seen me; will I be able to establish a bond with this innocent child? How will I take her from her current guardians? Most importantly, even if everything works in my favour, how will I succeed in bringing her up as her mother?*

The train reached Durgapur Junction at the right time and she came out and stood in front of the busy railway station. A multitude of commuters hurried hither and thither. The rush of office-goers returning from work was yet to start. She walked down to a nearby taxi stand and hired a cab after negotiating an affordable rate for an entire evening.

Savitri sat on the backseat and instructed, 'I want to visit orphanages or childcare centres around the city. I am a journalist and working on a documentary. Take me to every big and small organization here.'

The taxi driver, Naresh Halder, started the car and replied with a grin, 'I am a resident of this town since birth, Ma'am. I have lived here for the past fifty years! I think, with my experience, I know all the places that you would want to visit.'

'Do you know of a place called Haldi Kund?' enquired Savitri with the hope that he did.

Naresh Halder thought for a while and said, 'No, Ma'am. Never heard of that name.'

For the next four hours, Savitri visited about eleven different organizations that were either orphanages or childcare centres in

Epilogue

all corners of Durgapur. Beginning with the Durgapur Station Bazaar to the farthest corners of the industrial areas, Naresh Halder patiently drove his cab and took Savitri to almost every possible place known to him.

At every stop, Savitri searched for Devi or for a vague link with Arun or Radha but to no avail. She remained careful so as to not raise an alarm, and carried a nonchalant approach while meticulously looking for Devi. She interviewed the staff and tried to dig up some clue that could take her to Devi. However, her every effort was rendered fruitless and futile. She started to feel frustrated and heartbroken and was slowly losing hope.

As it was nearing almost 9.00 p.m., Savitri said to Naresh, 'Please take me to a decent hotel near the railway station where I can spend the night. It is getting late and I don't think we can find more places…'

Naresh replied, 'Ma'am, there are two more orphanages in Durgapur. I can vouch for it! You seem a bit dissatisfied with your trip and look tired. Let me take you to the Orient Star Hotel near the station. It is the best hotel in this town. If you wish, I will come back tomorrow morning and take you to those two places and then drop you at the railway station.'

Savitri replied wearily, 'Dada, you have helped me a lot. Please come back and pick me up tomorrow around 8.30 in the morning.'

That night Savitri managed to get a room at the Orient Star Hotel. She was tired and had a quick dinner and went to bed early. However, despite the tiredness, she felt a strange discomfort and her sleep was disturbed with intermittent spells of haunting dreams. One time, she dreamt of Arun and Radha, then she dreamt of a dark mist surrounding her as she roamed pointlessly through an empty street and finally she dreamt of Devi as she cried despondently and raised her hands in despair. Savitri sat up on her bed, breathing heavily and sweating profusely. Trying to calm down, Savitri drank some water and went back to bed.

The next morning, she got ready and came down to the reception desk to make the payment. Sharp at 8.30 a.m., Naresh Halder arrived and she got inside the cab quickly. He drove the cab to two more places at the farthest eastern boundary of Durgapur city, but Savitri's luck still did not favour her. She despaired, *Devi, my child, how will I find you? Where will I find you?* She looked up at the sky and prayed. She stood there helpless. After returning to the cab, she asked Naresh to take her back to the railway station.

Perhaps, I need to think more, Savitri thought. *Maybe, I need to ponder more and then come back after a few days.* As the cab drove past the roads and headed back, Naresh said, 'Ma'am, before you return, you must visit the famous Spice House of Durgapur. You had a hectic schedule, but I assure you that a trip to the Spice House will lift your spirit. The next train to Kolkata is around three in the afternoon. Let me take you to the Spice House, it will definitely be a refreshing visit for you!'

Savitri looked at her watch and saw that she had ample time at hand. To relieve her anxiety, she agreed and said, 'Alright Naresh dada, take me to the Spice House.'

Epilogue

Naresh smiled and replied while driving, 'Ma'am, the Spice House is not only an establishment of our local cottage industry, it has a vivid history! Some of the famous rebels during the Naxalite Movement used to take shelter in this place and hide their weapons too! It is a place that witnessed many gory encounters. Now, the place is run by a group of women led by Amma, the octogenarian lady who is the daughter of the original owner of the spice factory. They export their goods to many foreign countries as well.'

Savitri felt interested and sat back. The car drove for another half an hour and arrived in front of a yellow coloured three-storied house inside a moderate sized alley.

Naresh said, 'Ma'am, we have arrived. You can enter through that gate and ask for Amma. Trust me, you will enjoy your short trip here…'

Savitri got down and went inside through the open gate. She felt a bit uncomfortable to visit the house, which otherwise seemed completely devoid of human presence. As she passed by a few rooms, Savitri came to an open courtyard. On the opposite end of the courtyard, in front of an open door, a woman sat at a desk surrounded by heaps of paperwork.

She looked at Savitri inquisitively. The latter introduced herself, 'My name is Savitri and I am a visitor in Durgapur. I came here to take a look at your famous Spice House and meet Amma…'

The middle-aged woman took a thorough look at Savitri and then replied, 'Please wait a while here, I will inform Amma.'

Savitri waited at a corner of the courtyard for the next few minutes. The air carried a strong smell of spice. A few other rooms around the courtyard looked like storage rooms for spices. She could hear voices of men and women from different parts of the house, but could not see anybody.

Presently, an elderly woman slowly walked up to her from an adjacent room. She had a serene face and a fair complexion. Her white hair was long and well kept. Her skin had crumpled with age, but her smile carried an innocent sweetness with an angelic appearance.

The woman walked up to Savitri and softly said, 'I am Amma. How can I help you, my child?'

Savitri replied, 'My name is Savitri. I am a journalist by profession. I was visiting Durgapur for some work when my taxi driver, Naresh dada, mentioned about this Spice House.'

Amma looked at Savitri's face patiently for some time and then smilingly said, 'Savitri, you have taken a wise decision to come here. The Spice House has a mystic past and a promising present. It has something to offer to everybody! Come, I will show you around...'

Savitri liked the appearance and persona of Amma, and followed her obediently. The two of them walked past many rooms, numerous corridors spread across the three floors and Savitri saw how the Spice House was operated by the ladies in every aspect of the factory, starting from production to selling. Savitri was enthralled by the sheer expertise of all the women who were super energetic and performed their duties so diligently.

Epilogue

As the two of them came up to the roof, Amma said, 'Are you not the journalist Savitri, from the *Kolkata Chronicle*, who was covering the recent ruckus in Kolkata during Durga Puja?'

Savitri felt a bit awkward at this sudden recognition and replied softly, 'Yes Amma. You are correct. I am Savitri, the journalist. However, I have left my job. My involvement with the case earned me a bad name, even though I had supported the truth and the person whom I trusted and loved the most! I do not work in the media anymore… I am yet to figure out what I will do next in life. I have come to Durgapur for self-discovery, to gain inner peace that I seek to fill the void in my heart.'

Looking at her brimming eyes, Amma held her hands and softly said, 'Let me give you a little history lesson. Do you know what the Spice House was known as during the Naxalite movement? My father was the owner of this establishment and he had fondly given it the name…Haldi Kund!'

Savitri shuddered with shock as if she had been struck by lightning! She was unable to believe what she was hearing. She felt as if the entire world was spinning and she would faint any minute. A serene smile appeared on Amma's face as she stared at her. Before Savitri could speak, Amma pulled her by her hand and took her towards a room on the roof. She knocked on the door and a middle-aged woman opened it. Amma took Savitri inside.

Just as her pupils adjusted to the light inside the room, Savitri saw a girl sleeping innocently on a large wooden bedstead. Her eyes were fixed on the face of the little girl and she could only utter an ecstatic, 'Devi...is that you, Devi?'

Amma smiled and replied, 'Yes Savitri. She is indeed Devi, the daughter of Arun Palit! She is Devi, who has been awaiting her mother!'

Savitri looked at Amma with a perplexed look and questioned, 'How? Who are you? How did you know I am supposed to come? I am completely confused!'

Amma said serenely, 'Arun was my distant nephew. His parents passed away many years ago and I was his only kin left. From his childhood, he was very fond of me and his parents would bring him here during his winter vacations. As he grew up, he became a fine gentleman and an excellent officer. He married his love, the beautiful Radha, whom I had met only once. However, evil people destroyed his life! I still remember the night, when a despondent Arun had come to me with this beautiful child and handed her over to me. He had wanted me to hide her from the whole world and protect her! I looked at the little infant and looked into her eyes. They were searching for somebody...perhaps her mother! Till this day, her eyes carry that sadness as if she still seeks her mother silently. I feel so helpless looking at the child.'

Savitri's eyes were brimming as Amma continued, 'After he left, I kept reading the newspapers and followed the television media about the Devi case. I understood it was Arun who was taking revenge and I could also understand who he was referring to by the word "Devi". I refrained from calling the child by that name... So, I gave her a new name, "Durga"! She

Epilogue

is a special child who craves love and only love! I don't know how long I will live and how long I can protect her, and I pray she remains safe forever! Inside Haldi Kund, she is safe, but I don't know what will happen after I am gone! Durga's fate is uncertain. There is nobody to protect her after me!'

Savitri was crying profusely as Amma spoke, 'A few days later, during Durga Puja, Arun came here one night and showed me your photograph. He told me about you and your unconditional love for Arun! He told me that soon you will come for the child! Arun told me that even if he is no more, you will be there to protect this child… I didn't understand what he was trying to say. However, the incident of Maha Dashami made me understand what he was trying to say. Ever since that day, I had been waiting for your arrival…'

Savitri wiped off her tears and said, 'Yes Amma… I have come for her! This was my last duty that I had to fulfil. I will protect her forever! I will adopt her.'

Amma replied, 'I don't think that will be a problem. I will use my contacts to complete the formalities. Now come. As soon as she wakes up, you can meet her. Arun had left all necessary documents with me. The adoption process should not be difficult. I am happy that you have arrived. I can now die peacefully.'

Savitri looked at Amma and said questioningly, 'Devi has never seen me. She doesn't know who I am. Will she agree to come with me? Amma, will I be able to win her heart?'

Amma didn't answer; she patted on Savitri's shoulder and

tried to soothe her and then quietly walked out from the room. Just as Savitri turned to leave, she heard a voice. Devi had woken up from her sleep. It was not her usual time to wake up. She sat up on the bed, wiped her sleepy eyes and stared at Savitri. There was a thirst for love that melted Savitri's heart and she felt like running and hugging her. Caught up in the emotional turmoil, she was unable to move and so she sat down on the floor and wept.

In that untimely awakening, the innocent Devi blinked at Savitri and cried out loud with wide open arms, 'Maa…!'

The middle-aged woman in the room exclaimed, 'Amma! Did you hear that? She just said the word!'

Amma was smiling with ecstatic tears, 'Savitri, your question has been answered! Durga has spoken… She has found in you what her eyes have been seeking since birth! It's a divine intervention!'

'Yes!' sobbed Savitri and got up and hugged Devi. 'I have come, my child! I will never leave you.'

The innocent Devi kissed her chosen mother and with a smile, said again, 'Maa!'

Acknowledgements

A heartfelt thank you to my entire family for being my constant support system. I must mention that you have been a continuous support for all my work. Without your presence and inspiration, I am always incomplete.

Special thanks to the team at The Book Bakers, one of the leading literary agencies in the country today, for believing in my work. I thank you for shaping up my literary journey over the years and for motivating me to experiment with different literary styles. My literary agent Suhail Mathur has been one person who has always had faith in my writing, especially this manuscript. I feel fortunate to be associated with him and his team. Suhail has been a friend, a brother and a guide to me.

My sincere thanks to my publisher, Rupa Publications, for the undeterred faith in this book and in all my previous books too. Finally, I would like to thank my dynamic editor, Ms Saswati Bora, for her personal commitment and expert touch, and for trusting me and this book. Thank you Saswati for your dedication in refining this manuscript to its best shape.